This book is a work of fiction. Names, characters, events, places, and incidents either are products of the author's imagination or are used fictitiously. Any resemblance to actual events, locales, acquaintances (persons), living or dead, past or present, is entirely coincidental.

*Copyright © 2014 by Bianca Harrison*
*All rights reserved, including the right of reproduction of this book in whole or partial in any form.*

*Designed by Edifyin Graphix*
*Title page photograph © Nicholas and Gisela Johnson*

ISBN-13: 978-1502438089

www.authorbiancaharrison.com
https://twitter.com/mrsjanielle
https://facebook.com/authorbiancaharrison
instagram.com/mrsjanielle

Bianca
Harrison

# Love and War

## Dedicated To:

*Catherine Pack*

*Rachael Yvonne Pack*

*Mammie Johnson*

*Barbara Brown*

*Mary Hayes*

*Elizabeth Meadows*

*Betty Henderson*

*Love and War*

## **Anything Goes**

*A*va was laughing and drinking uncontrollably just to keep her sanity due to the men that were dancing all over the place. A 215-pound of chocolate drop was straddling her in the chair she was sitting in and it took all she could to keep her hands to herself. The strip club Lisa selected was mad crazy. Men were everywhere and the women went wild. This girl's trip was ending on a very good note Ava had to admit; Cancun would always have a special place in her heart. Ava looked at Karen who was gripping some guy's ass and he was sweaty. *How nasty!* Ava thought to herself.

"Ava and Angela, you girls better let loose and get right," Lisa said, downing another shot of tequila while sucking on a lime.

Karen was the wild one out the bunch - tall, blonde, and fit; she was the life of the party and made sure where ever she went she was going to have a good time. Ava looked up and Karen was still gyrating on the same guy. She just *knew* Karen was going to screw him before the night was over.

Ava was enjoying herself to the max, but watching those male strippers made her horny and she couldn't wait to get back home to her husband, Ryan, who was all the chocolate a woman needed. Being married for thirteen-years had its ups and downs, but through it all, they still had a chemistry that no one could break.

"Ava," Angela called out. "No thinking about home while we're on vacation!" she said handing Ava a shot of tequila.

They both counted to three and rushed the shot down, chasing it with a shot of Hennessy; Lord knows Ava would be sick in the morning if she kept it up. Angela and Ava were the married ones of the bunch; Lisa was divorced, while Karen never made it to the altar. Well, she almost did, but ran out on the guy and never looked back. She still talks about it to this day; she says that she was too scared to marry since she's so independent.

Lisa came over and said she had a massive headache and was ready to go. They all needed to get back to the hotel and pack because their flight left tomorrow afternoon. Angela went looking for Karen and came back saying she couldn't find her. *This is so like Karen to pull this mess every time*, Ava thought.

"I bet she's somewhere fucking ole dude," Lisa said as they all looked at each other and laughed because they knew it was true.

*Glad I wore this dress with no panties,* Karen said to herself. Mr. Ridiculous, as he called himself, was tall, built, white, and just right. He pulled her into a closet and they went to work. He picked Karen up, spread her legs, and sucked all her juices. Karen pulled her dress over her head so she could be free. She kneeled before him taking all of him in, playing with the tip of his head with her tongue ring. He was moaning and groaning as Karen pulled on him, then he exploded in her mouth just like that. He caught his breath, picked her up, and pushed inside of Karen, bending his back just a little so she could ride him.

"Oooo weeeee," Karen said, "they don't call you Ridiculous for nothing."

A white stripper calling himself Ridiculous, now ain't that something? But he does have a dick the size of a foot long sub. He was pushing inside of her like it was his last piece of ass. Ridiculous turned Karen over and she bent over for him, putting her hands on the walls as he spread her legs further apart. Again, he entered Karen slowly. She felt him grind for a bit then he gyrated faster, making his balls slap against her ass. Oh, it felt so good. He pulled Karen's hair then fucked her harder, "Bitch, throw that pussy back," he said pushing harder.

Hell, Karen couldn't even feel her pussy the way he was going on, it felt good at first then the fucking started to feel like a beating.

"I'm cumming," he said, still pushing deeper. "I'm cumin....ahhhh," he pulled out then took a deep breath.

"Did you cum? Ridiculous asked Karen.

Karen grabbed her dress off the floor, put it on and said, "Hell, no!" Then, she left the closet with him still trying to catch his breath.

*Damn*, she thought. *His ass had a big dick, but didn't know how to use it. What a waste*! She needed more shots to forget about what just happened. Karen straightened her dress, shook her hair, and headed back to the scene of things. Not wanting the girls to know where she had been, Karen mixed herself with the crowd on the dance floor until one of the girls came looking for her. After fifteen minutes of looking crazy on the dance floor, Karen noticed Ava heading her way, so she danced like hell.

"Karen," Ava called out then tapped her on the shoulder.

"Ava, what's up?" Karen said.

"Lisa has a headache and we're all ready to bounce, so let's go," she said pulling Karen away. "And by the way where the hell have you been because we looked all over for you!"

"Well, you all didn't look hard enough."

They both approached Lisa and Angela who were both standing by the door. "Miss Thang, we looked all over for you," Angela said as they started walking out the club.

"I was on the dance floor while y'all acted like Debbie downers," Karen said.

"Bitch, please. I saw your ass emerge from the back with that nasty ass stripper," Lisa said.

"You fucked him didn't you, Karen?" Ava asked.

Karen looked at her and burst out laughing, "What happens in Cancun stays in Cancun," she said.

"Yeah, but that don't mean bring anything back from Cancun as well!" Lisa said adding in her two cents.

They had hired a driver, so they jumped into the car and, instead of heading to the room, they stopped at IHOP. They were all hungry. Karen noticed a couple of guys she saw at the club approaching them saying something about a party, and she quickly said that they would be there.

Angela and Ava told the guys they were going to pass because it was going on 4:00 a.m. and they needed to rest before they left this place. Shit. Karen figured she could sleep when she got back; she worked Monday through Friday and sometimes Saturday. She lived for a good party.

Ava was already nodding off and the food hadn't even arrived yet. "Wake your ass up!" Lisa said after taking several Tylenol tablets for her headache.

Ava jumped just when their food arrived and they all ate in a hurry. Karen noticed Ava had barely touched her food, and asked Ava for her pancakes. Ava told Karen to go ahead, she didn't have an appetite - that she felt bloated and had gas. Karen didn't care. Hell she was hungry after all that alcohol she drank.

The four ended up passing on the party, and headed back to their rooms. It was now 5:00 a.m., and everyone started to pack before lying down. Karen just threw her clothes in her luggage and passed out.

It felt like Karen had just lied down and it was 12:30 p.m. Their flight left at 2:00 p.m. Ava was feeling discomfort in her abdominal area and still felt bloated. Ava was already on her period, so she just took a Midol to relieve the pain. Ready to get home, Ava tried to call Ryan several times, but he didn't pick up. She left him a message to say she'd be home in a couple of hours and hung up. Angela told Ava that she had spoken to her husband, Carl, and told him they would be home soon.

"At least you talked to your husband. I couldn't get mine to pick up," Ava said.

"He's probably in a meeting," Angela said as they headed out with their luggage. Lisa and Karen were behind still sleep walking with their sunglasses on. The breeze from the beach felt good on Karen's skin. Ava looked at the area once more before getting into the car.

They had a first class flight, which was nice; they all agreed that the next time they went on an all girl's trip, it would be in style. Those margaritas were definitely on point! Karen finally woke up after having several drinks. They all laughed, talked, and promised to always be there for each other no matter what. As they drifted through the clouds, Lisa took them back to Jamaica, the last trip they all took together. Angela and Karen laughed the longest, while Ava smiled, and then laid her head back in her seat. She was tired and had no energy. Finally they were able to relax as they enjoyed their flight back to reality.

## *The Beginning of an Era*

*A*va finally arrived home and sat down for a brief moment before she started to unpack. It was 7:00 p.m. and no one was home yet. Ryan was picking up the kids from her sister's house in the evenings while she was away. Ava picked up the phone and started to dial Ryan since she hadn't heard from him.

"Hi, babe," he said answering Ava call.

"Hi, sweetheart! Where are you guys? I'm finally home," she said.

"Glad you made it back safely. I'm actually headed over to your sister's to pick up the kids. I had a meeting that ran over and will be home shortly," Ryan said.

"Oh, okay...I'll see you guys in a bit," Ava said, ending the call.

Ava then decided to call her sister, Alisse; she felt some kind of way because Ryan didn't seem excited to hear from her at all. Ava brushed it off, then speed dialed Alisse.

*Love and War*

"Hey sugarfoot," Alisse said as she calls Ava sometimes.

"Hi, sis! What's going on? Are the kids there?" she asked.

"Yes, they've been here late since you've been gone. Ryan stated he had meetings and deadlines for things, so auntie Alisse been handling your job," she said laughing.

Ava loved her sister. Even though they were three years apart, they were very close. Alisse loved her niece and nephew and spoiled them every chance she got. She was engaged with no kids, but wanted to start a family of her own soon - as soon as she tied the knot.

"Abbie! Jaxon! Mommy Ava is home and she's on the phone," Alisse called out to them.

Ava heard screams in the background, "Yes!" Ava heard Jaxon say. He was a mama's boy. Alisse came back to the phone and said that Ryan just arrived and they should be home shortly.

Ava decided to get up, unpack, and soak before everyone arrived home. Shortly after she climbed out of the tub, the house went from quiet to noisy. "Jaxon, give it here!" Abbie said to her brother. *Lord, they were at it again*, Ava thought. Abbie was 12 and Jaxon was 11 and both were her pride and joy. As soon as they noticed Ava watching them, they ran to her and fell in her arms.

"Mommy, we missed you! What did you bring us back?" Abbie said, looking around the room.

"Nothing, but me," Ava said.

"You always bring us something back from your trips, so where is it?" Jaxon said grinning.

Ava told the kids to look in the bag next to her bed. They each had one with their name on it. After the kids ran from the room to chase down their gifts, Ava noticed Ryan checking the mail. She walked over and kissed him.

"Babe, I missed you," he said as he handed her a single rose.

"I missed you more," she said, wondering why he seemed distant.

"Tell me all about your trip," he said.

Ava told him about the trip, sharing that she had a wonderful time and would love to go back with him. Ryan looked very tired and Ava offered to give him a back rub. He told her maybe later. They did talk about Abbie getting into it with a girl at school because the girl called Abbie out her name; he had to go to the school and handle it.

Ava called Abbie to come down and asked her what happened. Both of her kids were in middle school and Ava found out that some kids are just mean. Abbie told Ava that a black girl got mad with her because the boy the girl liked had an interest in Abbie as well. The girl started picking on Abbie and called her white trash. Your dad married trailer park trash; you *think* you're black; your dad's sleeping with the help; and some other racist

*Love and War*

remarks. Abbie said when she got tired of it, she smacked the girl to show her how black she was and then they went at it.

Ava knew that she and Ryan would one day have this problem. They always tried to talk to their kids about their heritage. Ava fell in love with Ryan because of who he was, not his color. Although Ava is white and Ryan is black, she had always had issues with black women giving her the side eye whenever they were out. Their kids were biracial and they didn't care because they had parents who loved them.

Ava wasn't upset; she was glad Abbie smacked the little girl. Now maybe she knows to keep her mouth shut! Abbie was just like Ava, they take no mess. Ryan called Jaxon down and they both talked to the kids together. Ava and Ryan told the kids that they have to learn that words don't hurt anyone; not everyone was going to be nice, but that's life. Abbie got suspended for a day. Usually Ava would have been upset, but instead she hugged her.

The kids went upstairs and Ava poured Ryan a glass of wine. The kids had already eaten with Alisse and Ryan had grabbed a bite earlier. She gave him a massage, and then rubbed his feet. Ryan apologized for acting distant, he was just tired. Ava knew her husband and he wasn't himself. He was the financial controller of a large firm, which could be stressful at times. Ryan pulled Ava up close to him and held her in his arms. He was muscular and loved to work out, caramel, as she calls it, like Blair Underwood, and loved himself some Ava.

"Babe, you know, when I met you years ago at the bank, who would have known you'd be my wife," he said smiling.

"Me," Ava said remembering that day like it was yesterday.

Ava was the assistant manager for a large bank across town. She met Ryan when he came in wanting to talk about their business account. They went into her office and he just stared at her while she accessed his company account. She wondered why he said that she reminded him of Eva Mendes, the actress. It was flattering coming from a black man, but Ava got that a lot. After talking and helping him with what he had come in for, Ryan asked her out. From that day on the two were inseparable.

Ava looked at Ryan and kissed him, then laid her head on his chest.

"Babe, why don't you go upstairs and put on something sexy for me?" he asked, whispering in Ava's ear.

"Ryan, as bad as I want to make love to you, my period is on," she said while stroking him.

Ryan just looked at her, "Damn, Ava your period is always on, you need to get that checked out," he said moving her hand. "I get the feeling sometimes you don't want to make love to me," he added.

"Baby, it's not that! I have no control over what happens with my body. I'm sorry, but I can give you oral satisfaction," Ava said winking at him.

"I'll be upstairs," he said, as he got up and left.

*Love and War*

Ava went to check on the kids and told them to get ready for bed because it was late. She checked up on Ryan, who turned off his phone and got in bed. She laid beside him and apologized again for not being able to cater to him like he wanted. Ava started planting kisses on his chest as she made her way to his erection. He pulled her up and said, "Not tonight."

Feeling rejected, Ava simply laid on her side of the bed. Ryan turned his back to her, laid on his side, and went to sleep. As she tried to figure out what just happened, Ava laid in the dark hoping that whatever it was would pass.

*Bianca Harrison*

## *Bad Bitches*

$A$ngela got up early and made breakfast for Carl and Chrissy.

After a long flight back, she was taking an extra day off to rest. Angela was a dental hygienist with her own practice and has several other dentists that worked with her. So, being the boss, she could take off whenever she liked.

It was going on 6:00 a.m., and Angela went to wake Chrissy so she could get ready for school. Chrissy was thirteen and very prissy, which meant it took her longer to get ready.

"Mom, turn off the light!" Chrissy hollered.

Angela went in to check on Carl to make sure he was up, but he wanted her to come back to bed instead. Angela knew what he wanted, so she threw her gown across the bed and hopped back in. Serving her man before work gave him a big ego.

After lovemaking, they laid together for a bit before he decided to get up and shower. Angela joined him in the shower as she hurried to make sure Carl and Chrissy were fed and out the

## Love and War

door. She yelled for Chrissy to hurry up since Carl was dropping her off. Once the crew left, Angela cleaned the kitchen, turned off her phone, and headed back to bed.

After hours into her deep sleep, the home phone rang. *"Dammit,"* she thought. Angela forgot to turn the home phone off, too. Angela decided not to answer. She thought it was those damn telemarketers. But when she looked at the phone, she saw it was Ava calling.

"Ava, what's the problem?" Angela said in her rhapsody voice.

"Good morning to you. I knew you were off, so I wanted to do lunch," Ava said.

"Bitch, I'm sleep and you're talking about food. See you white girls get up too early…us black people, we like to sleep." Angela said.

"Yeah, yeah, yeah…and you're my black BFF, so get your ass up," Ava said laughing like hell.

Angela remembered meeting Ava years ago when she came into the dentist office Angela worked at, and ever since then they just clicked. Ryan helped Carl get a job at his company dealing with petroleum and they both have been very successful.

"Today was my rest day, what you have in mind? Angela asked.

"How about Neko's Lobster Bar? My treat," Ava said.

"Hell, yeah, give me a couple of hours. I'll meet you there. A sister loves free food," Angela said laughing.

"I thought so," Ava said hanging up.

Angela finally got up and got herself together. It was a pretty day outside, so she threw on her Chanel slippers, a fitted sundress, put her hair in a bun, donned her Chanel shades, and jumped in her Acura MDX.

Angela drove for about twenty-minutes. When she arrived at Neko's, she gave her keys to the gentleman to park her car in valet. He gave Angela a hard stern look as she walked to the entrance. Angela then turned around because she felt him looking at her.

"I know I look good," Angela yelled at the young guy as he smiled while she laughed. For a 39-year-old knocking on 40, Angela looked and felt like she was 20 years old. Angela stayed in shape, ate healthy at times, and was still in her prime. She could still drop it like it's HOTT.

Angela approached Ava, who always wore the finest attire like she was really Eva Mendes, but that was her girl.

"What's up, chic?" Ava said as she stood up and greeted Angela with her Michael Kors jumpsuit on.

"You look good," Ava said.

"Hell, I was trying to outdo you, but I see your ass out did me with your Michael Kors attire…and I love the watch!" Angela said.

"Girl, stop. Don't go there. We some bad bitches," Ava said.

"No doubt, we have expensive taste," Angela said.

The waiter came over and took their orders, it was after 1 p.m., so it was safe to order a martini. *Don't want to be called a drunk by ordering alcohol before noon*, Angela thought. Ava handed the waiter their menus and then headed to the bar. Angela was right behind her as they got their food and sat down.

"So, girl what did Ryan have to say about our l'il trip to Cancun when you got back?" Angela asked Ava.

"Girl, nothing. He didn't ask much. It was like he didn't care if I was back or anything; he was acting shitty," she said.

Ava talked about Ryan wanting to make love, but she'd been bleeding on and off for weeks and having low back pains. He acted like an ass, like she was seeing someone else and didn't want to have sex with him.

"Girl, you need to see your gynecologist just to make sure nothing's wrong. I know you get the birth control shot and that could be it, but just go check it out," Angela said to Ava.

"Yeah, you're right," she said.

Ava was also pissed about the incident with Abbie at school and wondered how people could be so cruel.

Angela explained to Ava that color would always be an issue for some people, but Angela let her know that she loved her like a sister; shit, they went together like salt and pepper. "Hell,

Karen's white, Lisa's black, and that's what makes us a pack," Angela said as they both burst out laughing.

Karen called Angela's phone as soon as they calmed down. "Damn, Ava, this chic's ear was ringing," Angela said as she answered.

"What you doing on your day off?" Karen asked.

"I was planning on resting, but Ava called and bribed me to lunch," Angela said as Ava gave her the side eye.

"You two bitches are dining without me?" Karen yelled through the phone. "Wait till I tell Lisa we weren't invited," she said.

"Girl, stop," Angela said as Ava talked smack to Karen in the background.

The waiter came, took their dishes, and then left the bill on the table. Angela was still talking to Karen who was in her office yapping about nonsense. Ava paid the waiter and Angela left the tip.

"Karen, Karen," Angela said trying to get her to breathe in between her sentences. "Let me call you back when I'm done with Ava because I know you ain't doing a damn thing at that job."

"You better call back," Karen said then hung up.

Angela looked at Ava and shook her head. "Your girl is a live wire," Angela said. Ava looked at her phone now Karen was calling her. Ava shook her head and ignored her call.

"I'll deal with her later," Ava said laughing.

*Love and War*

    Angela glanced at her watch and told Ava she had to leave. She had a facial appointment that she made before she arrived at the restaurant. They hugged each other and Angela told Ava to make sure she called her gynecologist for an appointment. Ava promised that she would. She got her car from valet then left.

*Bianca Harrison*

## *It Is What It Is*

$A$va drove down I-60 trying to get to Evans Creek; she wanted to drop by Ryan's office to surprise him. Ava called Abbie to make sure she was okay because she didn't like to leave Abbie by herself for a long period of time. Abbie was at home because she was suspended from school; Ava gave her some chores to do before she left to meet Angela.

Abbie was fine, the alarm was on, and she was watching television. So, Ava stopped by the coffee shop and grabbed Ryan an orange crème pastry and an iced coffee he liked when the weather became warm. Ava drove ten more minutes before arriving at Ryan's office building. Ava had a pass so she buzzed herself in and took a few minutes to talk to Nicole who worked the front desk.

Ava walked to Ryan's office and got there just as a couple of guys were leaving. They all smiled as Ryan noticed Ava, then gave her a "what are you doing here?" look.

*Love and War*

"Hey, baby," Ava said.

"Hey," he said as he kissed her forehead. "Everything okay?" he asked.

"Yes, I brought you something," Ava said handing him the pastry and coffee walking past him through the office.

Ryan smiled and thanked Ava for the coffee and pastry. He hugged her while taking a bite out of the pastry.

"So, how's your day?" he asked.

"It's good. I had lunch with Angela, checked on Abbie, and now I'm here," Ava said.

"Babe, you know I don't like you leaving the kids at home by themselves just yet. You could have eaten with Angela another day and saw me at home later," Ryan said in a serious tone.

"Excuse me for wanting to surprise my husband. The kids are growing up, they're not home by themselves all the time, but once every blue moon," Ava said, getting pissed.

"Ava, I just don't..." Knock, knock. They both turned around.

"Excuse me, Ryan. I need you to sign off on this contract," said the woman in a form fitting dress showing off the curves she had. She walked over and gave Ryan a pen to sign the contract, touched his hand, smiled at him, and then twisted out the office.

"Who was that?" Ava asked, wondering why the woman looked past her.

"A buyer for one of our large gas stations," he said.

Ava grabbed Ryan's hand and asked him what was wrong; he said nothing was wrong as he sipped his coffee. He apologized for pissing her off about the kids being home alone, and then kissed her hands. Ava followed Ryan to some of his colleague's offices and spoke to them. Ava saw Carl and told him she just left Angela. He said, "I know," as they all talked. Then Ava decided she had to go. Ryan walked Ava out up front, kissed her, and said he'd see her shortly.

Ryan went back into his office as Sharon walked in and closed the door behind her.

"So, that's Ava," she said.

"Yes, that's Ava," he responded.

"What was she doing here?" Sharon asked.

"She just stopped by to surprise me, that's all," Ryan said, wondering what was up with all the questions.

"She's pretty for a white girl; she has expensive taste, I can tell. So do I," Sharon added.

Carl knocked as he walked in and dropped off a folder that contained contracts that needed signatures. He didn't look at Sharon or Ryan, just dropped the folder off and closed the door behind him.

*Love and War*

Sharon walked behind Carl and locked the door. She turned around to face Ryan, pulling up her dress revealing the red lace thong she had on. She walked towards Ryan, took his hand, and told him to squeeze her ass. She turned around, bent over the desk in front of Ryan, and demanded he enter her for a quickie. Nervous as hell while playing with fire, Ryan glanced at the door, looked out the window, and then looked at his watch.

"What are you going to do?" Sharon asked.

Ryan unzipped his pants and pulled them down. He moved her thong to the side, and fucked her over the desk. She had a big ass and knew how to throw it back. She liked to grind on his dick until he exploded. Ryan gripped her ass as he went deeper in her jewels. Ryan then pulled out of her as he spread her legs apart; he sucked all her juices while sticking his tongue in her pussy. Sharon exploded when he did that shit. Ryan entered her again, bending her all the way over as he pulled her hair and fucked her harder. Sharon begged Ryan to stop as he ignored her ass. *She wanted the dick, the dick she gets*, Ryan thought.

Sharon was out of breath, and Ryan heard another knock on the door.

"Yes?" Ryan hollered.

"Ryan, I need you in my office," Henry said.

"Give me a couple of minutes, on a conference call," Ryan shot back.

Ryan stood there as he heard Henry leave. Ryan was beyond scared, as Sharon turned around on her knees and took him in her mouth. She sucked his balls, played with the tip of his head, then sucked him until his seeds fell into her mouth. Ryan released and Sharon caught every drop of his semen.

Luckily Ryan kept wipes in his desk; he hurried and cleaned himself up, wiped down the desk, and told Sharon to hurry. She said she'd talk to him later, grabbed the folder she came in with, and let herself out. Ryan sprayed the room, and then dialed Henry's extension.

Grabbing a piece of gum out the drawer, Ryan took a notepad and pen then proceeded down the hall. He noticed Carl, who wanted to say something, but opted not to.

## *When Reality Sets In*

After a couple weeks of writing Ava finally finished her novel of what she titled, "*If This World Was Mine.*" Ava hit send on her laptop and forwarded it to her editor. This would be her fourth book published. Ava found a passion for writing while she worked at the bank and was able to quit once she got a publishing contract, which was a blessing because she could work from home and tend to her family more.

Ava pulled away from her desk to get a refill on coffee then sat on the couch to catch *The View*, but was interrupted when Lisa called.

"Hi, Missy. What's good?" Ava said.

"Nothing, sitting in this office ready to go," Lisa said.

Lisa was an office manager for a company downtown and, like Karen, she didn't do anything but give orders.

"You're always ready to go, but what's up with you? Karen told me about your new boo," Ava said.

"Her big ass mouth! Damn! Let me tell my own business. Anyway he's someone I've been seeing for a couple months, but I wanted to see where it was going before I said anything to you ladies," Lisa said.

"Well?" Ava said.

"We both want the same thing. We've both been married and divorced; and we both have a son. So, we're taking it slow, but it's been nice so far," Lisa said, sounding happy.

"Lisa, if you're happy, then I'm happy."

Lisa asked Ava has she seen her gynecologist about her issue since Angela mentioned it to her. Ava told her not yet since the bleeding stopped.

Although Ava was able to make love to Ryan last night after weeks, her insides still felt sore. Hopefully the pain was because she hasn't had sex in weeks.

Lisa had to go since people were coming into her office with issues. Ava hung up and lied back on the couch until the pain in her pelvis got the best of her. Ava decided to call Dr. Patel, her gynecologist, to see her that afternoon.

Ava phoned Ryan, who talked briefly, and asked him to meet her for lunch. He told her he couldn't meet because of a conflict he had with a conference call. She politely said, "Cool," and told him she'd see him this evening.

Ava then headed over to the doctor's office and knew the wait was going to be awhile, so she went prepared. Ava watched

*Love and War*

House Hunters on the television screen they had set up in the waiting area. She also noticed the lady that came into Ryan's office a couple of weeks ago at the sign in. The woman didn't notice as Ava watched the woman walk to the back.

"Ava Decree," the young nurse called.

Ava followed her to get her weight and blood pressure. Then they immediately went into a room where Ava got undressed and put on a gown. Minutes later Dr. Kumar Patel walked in with his assistant.

"It's good to see you, Ava. What kind of problems are we having?" he asked.

Ava explained to him about the abdominal pressure, bloating, and the lack of energy she experienced, the gas, the lengthy bleeding, and the pelvic pain. She went on about the bleeding and how it occurred.

Dr. Patel put on some gloves while his assistant made notes into the computer. Ava laid back and Dr. Patel began a pelvic examination. The pain was unbearable as he pushed, felt, moved around, and then stated he wanted to do an ultrasound. He felt tumors and needed to see how big they were.

Minutes later, an ultrasound technician came into the room with a machine, which the technician used to see Ava ovaries while Dr. Patel studied the ultrasound screen. This went on about fifteen minutes and Ava got nervous as she watched the technician and Dr. Patel look at each other.

"Dr. Patel, what's going on?" Ava asked, concerned.

"Ava, what we're looking at is epithelial tumors outside of your ovaries," Dr. Patel said, as the technician pointed on the screen.

"I'm afraid to say it, but it looks as though this might be a form of ovarian cancer. But, it can be treated with surgery," Dr. Patel said calmly.

"Cancer? What do you mean I have cancer?" Ava asked, sitting up suddenly. Dr. Patel touched her shoulder and told her to lie back down.

"It looks like Stage II, which is indicated by the tumors in your Fallopian tubes; it's serious but luckily we caught it before it spread any further. Ava, I suggest we schedule surgery immediately to remove both ovaries and your Fallopian tubes," he said.

Ava started crying after she heard all she could. "Ovarian cancer," she kept mumbling. "Why me?" Ava asked.

Dr. Patel explained that the symptoms she had were indicative of ovarian cancer. Typically, this kind of cancer was silent and can go on undetected because its symptoms mimic ovulation.

Ava told the doctor she wasn't going to accept that; she needed a second opinion. Ava went to change, and then told Dr. Patel she would call him to schedule surgery if the other doctor came back with the same diagnosis.

*Love and War*

"Ava, I've been your doctor for many years and I wouldn't lie to you about anything. I understand this news is devastating, but I want you to do what makes you feel better. Call me or my nurse so we can get your surgery on the list, we don't want to wait too long," he said.

Ava took her check out form, signed it, and left his office, only to end up in the bathroom crying.

Sharon called Ryan earlier to inform him that she saw Ava at the doctor's office and was hoping she wasn't pregnant. Ryan wanted to call Ava, but decided to wait and see what that was all about.

Ryan wrapped things up early at work, and then called Ava to check in so that he could head over to Sharon.

Driving to the next town outside of Chicago, Ryan arrived at Sharon's with a dozen roses. He met Sharon during a meeting last year and landed a major contract with her company. Sharon moved to the area less than two years ago with her nine-year-old daughter, Tiffany. He respected her as a single mother; she was cool, smart, sexy, and had a sense of humor.

Sharon opened the door to her lavish condo and beamed when she saw Ryan.

"These are for you, lovely," Ryan said, moving in to kiss Sharon.

"Thanks," she said as she took Ryan's hand and hugged him. Sharon had on a fitted dress that was banging.

"Where is Tiffany?" Ryan asked Sharon.

"She has piano lessons and will be home in a couple hours. I fixed dinner so I hope you're hungry," she said as she winked at Ryan and headed to the kitchen.

Ryan followed her as he poured them both a glass of Merlot she had on the counter. Sharon prepared the table as Ryan wrapped his arms around her waist and kissed her on her neck.

"You talk to Ava?" she asked.

"Not yet, but soon," Ryan said.

"She's not pregnant is she?" Sharon asked.

"No. Just because you saw her at the doctor's office doesn't mean she's pregnant. Besides she and I haven't had sex in awhile, she claims to always be on her period," he said.

Sharon turned around to Ryan and said she didn't want him to have sex with Ava at all. "When are you planning on leaving her or at least telling her about us?" Sharon said looking at Ryan.

"Soon, baby, soon. Just give me a little time to get things in order, move some things around, and I'm all yours," Ryan said.

Sharon kissed him and unbuttoned his shirt as she pulled him towards the kitchen chair. Ryan quickly pulled her dress over her head and my, my, my...the girl wasn't wearing anything

## Love and War

underneath. She had a fresh wax and left her heels on. Sharon stood in front of Ryan as she danced and touched her toes while Ryan buried his face in her ass. Sharon sat on Ryan with her back against his chest, facing forward, gyrating in slow motion. Ryan kissed her back as he felt himself releasing.

Ryan told Sharon to get up, but instead she kept gyrating on him making him explode inside of her. Ryan lifted her up and laid her on the table. He made love to her there, on the table, that sent dishes flying everywhere. Ryan gripped her breast as he sucked and nibbled them, one at a time. Sharon was amazing and made him feel good...something Ava wasn't able to do like she once did.

Shortly after lovemaking, Ryan found himself wiping Sharon down in her hot tub. He relaxed and imagined a life with her. After kissing and nibbling on her ear, they heard a knock on the door and saw Tiffany, who closed her eyes and apologized.

"Sorry, Mom. Hi, daddy Ryan," she said and giggled.

"Hi, Tiffany," they both said in harmony.

"What are you doing here so soon? I thought you would call on your way home," Sharon said.

"Mom, I did call, but you didn't answer. Practice ended early because Ms. Logan had an emergency. And besides, I'm hungry," Tiffany said with attitude.

"Go to your room. Let me get out the tub, then I'll fix you something to eat," Sharon said.

Tiffany did as she was told; they dried themselves off, put on their clothes, and headed downstairs. Ryan picked up the dishes from the floor, and then ate a bit so he could hurry home.

Ryan glanced at the time, and noticed that it was his usual time to arrive home. He said goodbye to Tiffany and kissed Sharon goodbye. Ryan hated to leave, but didn't want to cause problems at home just yet. He wondered how he was going to ask Ava for a divorce, since he didn't love her anymore.

## When all Else Fails

Ava had an appointment with Dr. Ian Baker, a gynecologist who confirmed Dr. Patel's diagnosis. Doctor Baker also suggested Ava have the surgery to prevent any spreading and to cut out the cancer. Ava was devastated and at a loss for words. She called her mom and sister, Alisse prior, who both went with her to the doctor. Ava asked them both not to say anything to anyone including Ryan or the kids because she didn't want them to be concerned or worry.

"Ava, what are you planning on telling Ryan?" Alisse asked.

"I don't know, maybe I need to have a hysterectomy," Ava said, wiping her eyes.

Ava's mom squeezed her tight and told her everything would be all right. Alisse took her hand and hugged her. Ava scheduled her surgery for the following day. Then, she ran errands, picked up take out, and headed home.

Ava had so much going on through her mind, her agent called several times. Ava called her to explain her situation and that they needed to push the book release back for a couple more weeks. Ava's agent wasn't pleased because of the budget, but understood the circumstances. Ava then called Angela while she waited on Ryan to arrive home. She would talk with him and the kids together.

When Angela picked up, Ava just cried until Angela asked what was wrong. Ava told her about her surgery, but ended up telling her about the cancer. Ava swore Angela to secrecy and promised not to say anything as bad as it hurts.

"Ava, I'm glad you went to the doctor. I just knew something wasn't right," Angela said.

Angela comforted Ava the best she knew how and promised to be by her side every step of the way. Ryan walked in and looked at Ava; he asked, "What's wrong?"

"Angela, I have to go, talk later," Ava said and hung up.

Ava ran into Ryan's arms and hugged him tight. "Babe, what's going on, you've been crying," he asked.

"Jaxon, Abbie, please come down," Ava called out.

Ava sat everyone down then explained about her symptoms, the results of the tests, and then about the hysterectomy and the surgery. Ryan took Ava's hand and squeezed it as the kids hugged her. Ava made everything sound positive and explained that the surgery was a quick procedure.

## Love and War

The kids dismissed themselves while Ryan talked to Ava about the surgery. He said that he would accompany her and take care of the kids. Ava hugged Ryan, and then kissed him; she also noticed the make-up he had on his collar and the scent of perfume on his skin, but ignored it. Moments later Karen called, and then Lisa, who were both concerned about the surgery. Karen was dramatic while Lisa was over the top, a reason why Ava never told them anything. Ava knew Angela would call and tell them; it was cool. They were her girls. She just didn't want anyone to know that she actually had cancer and would beat it; Ava didn't want anyone to worry.

Ava went to talk to the kids in their rooms. Abbie was very sensitive and Ava explained that while she is in the hospital recovering from her surgery, Abbie would be the woman of the house. Ava told her to look after her brother. Ava told Jaxon the same thing - to take care of Abbie - and that he would be the man of the house while Ryan was away for any reason. She told them that she'd be home on recovery for four to six weeks and may be a little tired, but she expected them to carry their weight. Both kids understood and gave Ava the biggest hug ever. When all else failed, Ava always had her kids and no matter what, they would be taken care of.

Ava went to pack for the surgery and heard Ryan whispering on the phone. Ava was positive he was talking to someone he didn't want Ava to know about; she also felt that he was cheating on her, but didn't want to believe it. Ava did everything for Ryan and gave him everything he needed, so he didn't have a reason to cheat. Ava got on her knees and prayed before she turned in for the night.

---

After a sleepless night, Ava and Ryan decided to arrive at the hospital early for her surgery. They got the kids up to drop them off at Brian's house. Brian was a friend of Ryan's who offered to take the kids to school that morning. After she said goodbye to the kids, Ryan drove Ava to the hospital. She checked in and when she looked up she saw all her girls - Angela, Lisa, Karen, Alisse, and her mom, Elaine. Ava held back tears to keep from crying; Angela whispered to her that everything was going to be okay and she promised to be there. Ava also noticed Karen talking to Ryan and the conversation looked intense due to her facial expression and hand movements. When Ava called out for Ryan, he smiled and walked over.

Dr. Patel called for Ava and was ready to prep her for the procedure. After a couple hours of extensive surgery, the doctor moved Ava to a recovery room where he told her that everything went well and she should make a full recovery. He explained that, even though he was able to remove all the cancer and Ava's

*Love and War*

fallopian tubes, ovaries, and uterus, the cancer could always be in remission, which meant it could return at any time and she would need to undergo treatments of chemotherapy. Still drowsy, Ava told Dr. Patel prior about keeping her diagnosis confidential from her husband, friends, and family. She explained that they all thought she was there for a hysterectomy; so when he went into the waiting room, he explained as little as possible and noted that everything went smoothly with the surgery.

    Ryan came in and told her that everything went well. He was followed by Elaine, Alisse, and the girls. Ava was mentally drained and ready to go home; that evening, Ava was cleared to go home. Her blood pressure stayed normal and she was glad because Dr. Patel said her blood pressure went up during surgery. They wanted to keep an eye on it. Ryan drove Ava home and when they arrived, the kids had flowers and balloons everywhere. Alisse had come to the house before they got there and arranged everything, Abbie even tried to cook, and Ava gave her an 'E' for effort.

    Days passed following the surgery and everything went back to normal. Although Ava was moving in slow motion, her mom helped her a lot while Ryan worked. Every morning Ava's mom took her to her chemotherapy treatments without Ryan knowing, her mom didn't like it and felt like she needed to tell him, but she honored Ava wishes. The treatments made Ava tired, so she would sleep when she got back home following the appointments.

Ava's agent called as she planned to release her book in a few weeks and Ava wanted to get well, so she could do book signings. Ava started keeping a journal since the surgery so she could keep everything together as the days go by. Thinking back to the day of the surgery Ava dialed Karen, out of curiosity.

"Well, hello lady, how are you feeling?" Karen said when she answered.

"Hi, girl, I'm actually feeling better; taking it day by day," Ava said.

"Did you get my basket?" Karen asked.

"I did and thank you for the lovely treats. You know I loved it, it had all of my favorites and I really appreciate you being there during my surgery," Ava said.

"What are friends for? I don't have many friends, Ava, and you are like a sister to me and I love you," Karen said sounding all mushy.

"Karen...I also called for another reason, I saw you talking to Ryan at the hospital and you had your hand in his face. What was that all about?" Ava asked curious.

"Ava, Ava, Ava," she said.

Karen explained that, while she was out on a dinner date, she saw Ryan on the other side of town dining with some big booty tramp and her daughter. She made it known that she saw him and snapped a photo. She went on to tell Ava that she was so disgusted when she saw how chummy he was with the daughter, like he

*Love and War*

didn't have a family at home. And although she didn't make a scene, she went over and spoke to him. She could tell that his heart almost jumped out of his chest.

"I'm so sorry, Ava, I was going to tell you. I just needed to find the right time; especially since you were having surgery that morning. I confronted his ass and of course he said it was a business meeting and the lady just happened to bring her daughter along since she didn't have a sitter," Karen said.

"Thanks, Karen, I appreciate your friendship," Ava said as she held the phone.

"Ava, you there? Ava?" Karen called out over the phone.

Ava was so distraught she just sat there while the phone went into a tone of its own.

*Bianca Harrison*

## *Lies and Betrayal*

$F$inally Ava's book was being released, and companies were shipping out copies of it out as the orders came in. A lot of customers preordered their copy of "If This World Was Mine." It had been weeks since her surgery, and Ava felt better than ever; so much so that she gathered enough energy to throw a release party at the Coliseum.

The girls were just as excited as she was and pitched in to help with the party. Abbie was great - she designed a dress for Ava and made it, too. Ava promised Abbie that she would wear it to the party. Ryan acted as if everything was cool, which it was, but Ava knew all about his affair. Ava couldn't understand why he would cheat on her; just the thought depressed her every time she thought about it. Ava just tried to make it work.

Ava was heading over to Book Golure in the mall for a book signing with her agent and Karen. Karen apologized for hurting Ava with the news about Ryan, but Ava was just glad she told her. Ava told Karen everything was fine.

"Ava, we both love black men, although I will take what I can get," Karen said laughing. "But why are you putting up with Ryan's bullshit?" Karen asked.

Ava took Karen's hand and told her it was complicated.

"Ryan and I have kids together and I promised to death do us apart. I love Ryan. I'm not sure what it is; maybe he's going through a phase," Ava said, trying to reassure herself.

Karen hugged Ava and told her she was too pretty and sweet for any man to hurt her the way Ryan was.

Ava turned her head and wiped tears as they got out of the vehicle and went into the bookstore that had a line wrapped around the corner.

"OMG," Ava's agent said as she smiled at her.

"Is this for my book?" Ava said with enthusiasm.

This was Karen's first book signing event with Ava. For the others, she worked on the day of the book release, but this time, she took the day off. Karen was just as excited as Ava; she helped Ava set up and was ready to take photos for whoever wanted one with the author.

Hours into the event, Ava's eyes lit up when she saw Ryan in line with the kids and his book, which made her day. When Ryan approached the booth, Karen gave him attitude. Jaxon wanted a picture with his favorite author and they all took a family picture with her book.

"I'm proud of you," Ryan said.

"Thanks, babe, I'm proud of myself. Thank you for bringing the kids and showing support," Ava told him.

They left and the event continued until 6:00 p.m. Ava's agent booked more signings for her to do throughout the month and she was exhausted from those couple of hours. They had to hurry so she could get dressed and head to the party.

Hours later, Ava was heading to the party in her short mini gold metallic dress that Abbie designed. Ava took pictures and sent them to her. Abbie was ecstatic. Ava thought, *"This will make her go after her dream as a fashion designer. My baby got skills."*

Ava met Ryan at the entrance. As they went in, friends, family, colleagues, and several other authors Ava invited welcomed Ava and Ryan. She saw Angela and Lisa and thanked them for an amazing party, the decorations were sick. Ava was so happy as she and the girls took photos, danced, and, of course, Ava signed more books. She also read a couple of excerpts from her new novel and everyone was pleased.

Ava noticed Carl talking to Ryan as they walked towards the entrance. Ava motioned for Angela who came over; Ava then cut the signing short and asked her to take a walk with her. Angela looked confused as they headed towards the front as Carl was coming back in.

*Love and War*

"Ladies, don't you both look lovely," Carl said looking nervous.

"Thanks! Carl have you seen Ryan by any chance? Ava asked.

"Ryan went to the restroom," Carl said pointing in the opposite direction.

Still looking confused, Angela looked at Carl and said, "We'll be right back." Carl just stood there with his hand in his pocket. Ava got outside as people were still coming in and noticed Ryan arguing with the same lady from his office.

"Ryan!" Ava called out.

He turned around, looking like he saw a ghost; then he continued to talk to the lady as if Ava wasn't there.

"Who is she?" Angela asked.

"Not sure, but I'm about the find out," Ava said storming towards Ryan as he put the woman in a taxi and it drove off.

"Ryan, how dare you bring her here! This is my event and you flaunt your mistress," Ava said.

"Ava, let's go back inside and enjoy ourselves, we'll talk about it later," Ryan said feeling the heat on him.

"So, is it true? That woman is your mistress?" Ava asked.

Lisa ran out, asking where everyone was, as Ava was too upset to deal with anyone. She gathered herself together, walked past everyone, went up front, made a heartfelt speech, and thanked everyone for supporting her and coming out.

"Ava, are you okay?" Alisse asked.

"No, sis, Ryan's tramp was outside. So no, I'm not okay!" Ava said, about to break down.

"Sis, you stay here, I'm about the handle this!" Alisse said storming off.

Ava slipped out the back door, got into a taxi, and left. She cried hysterically on the way home. Ava couldn't believe Ryan would disrespect her like that.

---

When Angela and Carl arrived home, Angela asked Carl what the hell was going on with Ryan.

"Angela, I don't know what's going on, honestly," Carl said.

"Babe, you know something, you tried to keep us from going outside to see what he was up to," Angela shot back.

"Yes, I did. I didn't want any mess going on at Ava's event, that's all!" Carl said, trying to end the conversation.

Angela wanted to know more and needed to check on her girl. That shit Ryan pulled was foul. Angela picked up the phone and dialed Ava's number. Ava's phone went straight to voicemail. Angela tried several more times and got the same thing.

*Love and War*

"Hello?" Angela answered as her phone rung as soon as she put it down.

"Angela, have you heard from Ava? I'm worried about her," Lisa asked.

"Damn, Lisa I thought you were Ava calling back. I've been trying to reach her and her phone goes straight to voicemail," Angela said.

"I know! That's why I called you...hold on, Angela," Lisa said clicking over.

Carl walked back into the room. "Babe, can you call Ryan just to check on Ava?" Angela asked him.

"Girl, I'm sorry that was Karen," Lisa said clicking back over. "She is also concerned and thought about going over to Ava's, but I told her to hold off. Maybe she just needed time."

Lisa explained to Angela what Karen told her about running into Ryan with another woman and her daughter at the restaurant. Angela didn't understand, Ava never mentioned it and they are very close. Angela rushed Lisa off the phone so she could find out from Carl.

"Babe, is Ryan seeing anyone at the workplace?"

"Angela, again I don't know what's going on, let's just drop it!" He said.

Pissed, Angela just looked at Carl and said, "I hope he's not for his sake!"

45

Carl came out from the bathroom and shook his head. "Angela, let Ava and Ryan focus on their relationship, not you," he said.

Angela got up, kissed Carl goodnight, and got in bed without saying a word. She was simply upset how Ryan was trying to play her friend.

*Love and War*

## *Getting Through the Pain*

*A* couple of months after Ava's book release, she did a lot of touring to promote her book. It was her biggest best seller and had phenomenal sales in its first week. Traveling gave Ava some time to heal, pray, think, and take care of herself. She took the kids along on weekends to show them what she did and explained to them that hard work does pay off.

After the incident at Ava's book release party, she confronted Ryan, who stated that Sharon was just a fling. But Ava knew better because she followed him for a couple days just to see for herself and he was still seeing her.

Ava was confused, and most of all hurt, so she buried herself in her writing while trying to make her marriage work.

Ava finally got up, went to her closet, and pulled out a red and black jumpsuit that was sent to her as a gift by Osmane Yousefzadar, a well-known fashion designer out of London. She was a guest speaker at one of his events last year and he had been generous to her ever since.

Ava needed to hurry and get dressed because Alisse would be there soon. Ava was meeting the girls at Turnpike for a girl's night out to celebrate her success. She was really looking forward to it.

"Where are you headed to?" Ryan asked when he walked into the room.

"Out with the girls," Ava said.

"So, you don't want to chill with me? We could go out," he said.

Ava was taken back. Ryan hadn't said anything all day, but now seeing her getting dressed, he wanted Ava to change her plans.

"Sweetheart, we could go out tomorrow, just me and you."

"Ava, I want to go out tonight with you!" Ryan kept at it.

"Ryan, what is it? Do you not want me to be happy? Now you want to go out or is it you don't have plans with your whore tonight?" Ava asked not realizing what she just said.

"No, I don't. My whore gave me the night off to spend time with you," Ryan said as he stormed out the room.

"Asshole!" Ava yelled.

Not knowing why Ryan was so angry with her, Ava continued getting dressed, but couldn't get Ryan's recent behavior out her mind.

*Love and War*

Ava cherished Ryan and even made excuses as to why he was cheating on her. Ava even went to bat for him with her family because they didn't want her to marry him because he was black. But, when she did, they loved him just the same as any other. Ava stood up and felt a sudden pain in her lower stomach; she brushed it off as she heard Alisse call her from downstairs.

---

Arriving at Turnpike, the girls had a VIP section, which was nice. The girls looked stunning; Ava had also invited a few other friends as well, so the turnout was good.

Karen started popping bottles while Alisse started pouring.

Lisa got a cake made that read, "Congratulations to Our Favorite Author," and made a toast. All the girls gave wonderful speeches, and after three glasses of champagne, Ava was ready to turn up.

Lisa pulled Ava onto the dance floor, and she was feeling good. For a white girl with black friends, Ava could drop it like it's HOTT, thanks to Lisa and Angela. They jammed to 2 Chainz, *Future*, then the DJ played *Drunk in Love* by Beyonce. Ava looked over at the bar and noticed Ryan, Brian, and Andrew, one of Ryan's co-workers and close friend. Ryan was all up in some blonde's face and did not notice Ava; Ava turned around and continued dancing.

Some young hottie got behind her, touching Ava and grinding on her, so she went with the flow and gave him a show.

"Go Ava, go Ava," Karen said laughing and drunk.

Her friends watched Ava grind on the young buck and then back it up.

"That's what I'm talking about!" Lisa said, as she danced next to Ava with some guy. Everyone was having a good time, then all of a sudden Ryan came out on the dance floor and stood next to Ava.

"What the hell do you think you're doing?" Ryan said angry as hell.

"Dancing," Ava said turning around.

Ryan grabbed Ava's arm, "Let her go," Alisse said, pushing him. The guy she was dancing with was long gone.

"Ryan, why do you have to screw up everything?" Ava said yelling at him.

"My wife's out here dancing like a whore, like she's single, is not the business," he said.

"Ryan, what about you all up in that blonde's face at the bar? You act as though you're single and you're already cheating on me!" Ava said before Angela pulled her back to the VIP section.

Everyone was looking as Ryan caused a scene. Ava was so embarrassed that she was ready to leave.

"Ava not tonight, this is about you," Angela said.

*Love and War*

"Here take this shot," Angela said as they both took it to the head and laughed.

"Angela, you have no idea. Without my kids and y'all, I'll be a basket case," Ava said.

As the night ended, the girls were still upset by Ryan actions and Alisse didn't want Ava to go home. The kids were at her mom's, so *"Whatever happens, happens,"* Ava thought.

Returning home Ava noticed Ryan was already upstairs. She went to shower and heard the shower door open.

"Babe, I'm sorry, I had too much to drink," Ryan said. He stripped naked and got in the shower like everything was cool.

"What is going on with you, Ryan? I can't help you if you don't tell me," Ava said as water ran down her back.

"Nothing's wrong. I don't want to see anyone else all up on my woman," Ryan said, still sounding drunk.

"Yet another woman is sleeping with my husband," Ava said.

Ryan tried to kiss Ava's back as she pushed him off. "Babe, you're losing weight. Your booty is getting small," he said.

"Maybe you just haven't noticed me," she said hurt by what he just said.

"Ava, I love you," Ryan said as he kissed her and pushed her against the shower door. He caressed Ava as she gave in while he entered her. The sex was painful and boring. Something was going on with her husband and Ava was unsure if she could fix it.

*Bianca Harrison*

## ***Emotional Rollercoaster***

*T*hings seemed to be going smoothly for Ryan, who decided to make sure Ava was happy as well as Sharon, who was okay with his agreement for now. Ryan planned on being with Sharon, but needed time to do things the right way, especially for his kid's sake.

    Over the last couple of months Ava stabilized. She did whatever Ryan asked and more. Ryan knew Ava loved him like the sweat off his balls and he loved her, too; but, not like he used too. He thought that something was missing from their marriage; it was not what it used to be. He pitied Ava. Ryan felt happier with Sharon and adored her daughter, Tiffany.

    Thinking to himself, Ryan didn't know how Abbie would feel about Tiffany. Abbie was a daddy's girl and Ryan adored her just as much. Jaxon was his partner in crime, but was a mama's boy; he wouldn't do well with Sharon.

*Love and War*

Ryan seemed phased as he looked out his office window trying to figure out his next move. He heard a knock on the door and it was Andrew, who worked in the Purchasing Department.

"What's up, man?" Andrew said as he came over to shake Ryan's hand.

"Nothing man, just enjoying this view," Ryan responded.

"I saw your L'il shorty here earlier, you get some?" Andrew said laughing rather loudly.

"Man, what are you talking about?" Ryan said, acting stupid not trying to let anyone know about his business, not even Andrew. They were cool and hung out, but there were some things you kept to yourself until you were ready to reveal.

"Fine ass Sharon, who we got that major contract with, I heard you're hitting that," Andrew said while grinning.

"Man, I'm about business and she is, too. She's cool peeps," Ryan said smiling.

"Yeah, right. Ricky done hit that, so I know you have, too. You think I'm crazy? I know better because I'll be hitting that from the back all over that desk," Andrew said cracking up.

They both laughed at his assumptions. Andrew was wild and Ryan tried to hook him up with Karen, but she was dating someone at the time. Andrew also has a son the same age as Jaxon, which was good; they often took the boys places together.

"Let's do lunch, it's almost that time," Andrew said.

"Sure let me wrap up something and I'll meet you in the lobby, say in an hour," Ryan said. Andrew left the office and messed with everyone he saw floating in the hallway.

Thinking back to what Andrew said about Sharon screwing Ricky was news to him. She wasn't the type to give it up to anybody, but then again Ryan got it pretty easy. Puzzled, he sat and dialed Sharon's number.

"Well, hello there," Sharon said as she walked in Ryan's office with her phone in her hand looking at him.

Ryan hung the phone up and motioned for her to close the door. And, of course, she locked it. Sharon wore an ivory dress that flared right at the knees showing off her nicely toned legs. It hugged her body just right.

"Hi, sexy," Ryan said as he got up to kiss her. "I wasn't planning on seeing you here today, but heard you were in the building…what brings you by?"

"I had to meet with your sales department and dropped off some projections for Ricky," Sharon said.

"Ricky," which raised a brow for Ryan. "Sharon I need to ask you something and, babe, please be honest."

"What is it?"

"You fuck, Ricky?" he managed to ask her.

Looking at Ryan sideways she responded, "Yes, once. Which is in the past."

*Love and War*

"Damn! So I'm going behind Ricky with his hating ass?" Ryan said shocked at Sharon's response.

Sharon slapped the black off of him. "What did you do that for?" he said.

"You got some nerve! This was before us and it happened one time. I'm going behind Ava everyday, so until you leave her, then you can't question me," Sharon said as she made that clear.

Ryan apologized, but had so many questions at the same time. Ricky was a sneaky, hating ass dude. As bad as he wanted to rip Sharon's clothes off, he couldn't knowing that Ricky was probably banging her over his desk. Sharon assured Ryan that's all it was after she saw how concerned Ryan was, but he wasn't so sure.

"Dinner later?" Sharon asked.

"Yes," Ryan said. Sharon kissed him on the lips and strutted out the office.

---

Ryan was heading over to Sharon's when Ava called. "Babe, you didn't forget about Jaxon's baseball game, did you?" Ava asked.

"Shit!" Ryan mumbled. "I'm on my way, running behind," Ryan said turning around to go in the opposite direction.

Ryan quickly called Sharon and told her he couldn't make it, that he forgot all about Jaxon's game. She was a little upset, but understood he had to be there.

Getting to the game at the fifth inning, Ryan could tell that Ava and Jaxon were upset. "You just missed your son's home run," Ava said.

"I'm sorry, babe, I lost track of time. I'm here now," he said.

"Ryan, people make time for what's important to them, remember that!" she said with attitude.

"Not here, okay? Let's not go there."

The game went on and Ryan was proud of Jaxon, who played centerfield and could catch like Curtis Granderson. His team was number one in the nationals. Ava clapped and screamed while Abbie walked around with her friends.

The crowd was rowdy like these kids were playing for a major league team. Ryan guess he worked so much he didn't get a chance to see his kids enjoying what they like. Although he may have issues with Ava, she was a damn good mom. Even when she had places to be, events, book signings, she would catch the next flight to head home for any of the kids' games or recitals.

"Babe, I see you enjoying the game," Ryan said making conversation.

"This is what I do. There was a time when you enjoyed our kids as well," Ava said.

*Love and War*

    Ryan didn't respond back because she was right. How did he get to this place? He didn't know....Abbie walked up with one of her friends from school and spotted Ryan sitting next to Ava.

    "Dad! You made it!" Abbie said as if Ryan never made it to anything, which made him feel some type of way.

    "Yes, baby girl, I told you all I was coming, but nobody believed me," he said.

    Ava cut her eyes at Ryan, then turned her head. Ryan's phone vibrated several times as he looked at it and noticed it was Sharon texting him and sending Ryan sexual pictures of herself.

    One that read: *Baby see what your missing* as she posed in a zebra panty and bra set with her legs open and her hands on her crotch. The next picture came in with her topless covering her breast licking her lips.

    While Ryan gazed at the pictures Sharon sent, the crowd jumped as one of the boys on Jaxon's team hit another home run. The lady behind Ryan jumped and accidentally hit him causing his phone to fall out of his hand. Ryan went to pick it up, not finding where it landed, only to see Ava standing with his phone in her hand, looking at the text Sharon just sent.

    "It amazes me how some females can be so thirsty, Ryan. I never cheated on you and here you are putting your whore before your family," Ava said screaming at Ryan in front of the crowd. "How dare you," Ava said and stormed off.

    "Mom, what is it?" Abbie asked chasing Ava.

"Damn," Ryan said. Looking for his phone, that's when he saw Ava toss it in the trash.

Ryan ran to the trash can, dug in it, and got the phone out. Ryan walked and waited up front for the game to end so that he could congratulate Jaxon and leave.

"Good game, son," Ryan said to Jaxon, giving him a high five.

"Thanks, dad, glad you could make it, but you missed my home run," he said.

"Yeah, I'm sorry. I was getting here as fast as I could," Ryan responded.

With so much animosity in the air, Abbie nor Ava said a word. They all left talking amongst each other, but not acknowledging him.

Ryan contemplated going to Sharon's, but figured he'll just head home.

## A Fist Full of Tears

*W*riting used to be a hobby for Ava, now it had become her outlet. She wrote every chance she got. She became very successful with the sales of her books, writing for other people, and her speaking engagements. Ava was featured in Storme Magazine, a popular publication for entrepreneurs in a diverse culture who are working on a career in literature. She was proud of her accomplishments; she thought she would be stuck at that bank for the rest of her life.

    Breaking from her desk, Ava noticed a text from Ryan that read: *"How about lunch?"* Ava ignored it and walked outside on the patio to get some air. Ava thought about divorcing Ryan, but kept thinking about Abbie and Jaxon. Ava's father was horrible and left her mother when she put a bat to his ass and she never saw him again until he showed up at one of her book signings. She never mentioned it to her mom, only Alisse. They both liked to pretend that he was dead, so Ava didn't want her kids growing up without Ryan.

Ryan played games and Ava was his pawn because he knew she was vulnerable. But it wasn't just that: Ava didn't believe in divorce. As Ava thought, she made a couple of calls and set up a few appointments. She was not about to let Ryan take her money and use it on that tramp of his.

Ava kept looking at the pictures of Sharon, the ones she sent Ryan. Before she threw his phone in the trash, she forwarded the pictures to her phone.

"Look at this bitch, posing for a married man in her bra and panties. What make females go after men that are taken? That's so disrespectful," Ava said aloud, talking to herself.

Ava received another text from Ryan, "You ignoring me?"

Ava really didn't have time for his bullshit. She went back in and wrote some more before her thoughts of Ryan consumed her. It was almost lunchtime as she planned on meeting with the girls for lunch.

Ava stood up and felt her stomach cramping. She showered then dressed, as she brushed her hair down and left.

*Love and War*

Ava arrived at the spot where Lisa told her to meet them. As she walked inside, the waiter took her outside on the patio, "Hey, divas," Ava said as all the girls stood up and greeted one another.

"Oh my, Karen cut her hair? It looks good, chica!" Ava said.

"Yes, darling, I'm a brunette now," Karen said looking graceful.

"I like that on you. Wow! You look really young!" Ava said.

"We all like it," Lisa added.

"Well thank you all. My man likes it, too," Karen said.

"Spill it!" Angela hollered.

Karen told us about the guy she's been seeing and how she met him at a conference she attended for her job. So far things seemed to be going fairly well; the only thing was, he has a six-year-old daughter and he's a single parent - the little girl's mom died of breast cancer. But Karen loves the little girl to death.

"Aw, you'll be a great stepmom and a mom of your own," Lisa teased Karen and winked at her.

"You seem to like him. Give it a shot and don't run away this time girl!" Angela said as they all laughed.

The waiter brought them all water and appetizers that Karen ordered; then he sent over an apple martini from the bar and handed it to Ava.

"Sir, I didn't order this," Ava said.

"The gentleman at the bar did and told me to give it directly to you," the waiter said.

Everyone looked back and the guy waved walking towards the table. The girls had a field day with this because they knew what Ava was going through with Ryan and felt that she needed to give him a dose of his own medicine.

"Hi, ladies," the guy said turning his attention to Ava. "A beautiful drink for a beautiful lady. My name is Malcolm," he said reaching for Ava's hand.

"Malcolmmmmmm," Lisa said dragging his name out in laughter.

"I'm Ava," she said standing up, motioning for the guy to follow her inside away from the girls.

They both sat at the bar for a brief moment, enough for Malcolm to tell Ava he noticed her when she walked in and, of course, read her books. Ava had to quiz him on them just to see if he was lying, but he passed.

"I rarely find guys that read," Ava said.

He looked at Ava and said, "I'm not just any guy."

Ava smiled when he told her how beautiful she was in person.

*Love and War*

Malcolm was sweet; not really Ava's type, but he wasn't bad, either. He was smaller than Ryan, but had a nice tan complexion and was very clean cut. As they shook hands, Ava told him maybe they could have coffee one day. Malcolm gave Ava his business card as he smiled. She thanked him and walked back to the girls. He left a tip, then exited the restaurant.

"Don't even ask," Ava said to the girls, getting back to the table smiling.

"Well, if it doesn't work out with Ryan, then there goes your man. I see he made you smile," Lisa said.

"He was nice looking," Angela added.

"What's up with you and Ryan anyway?" Karen asked.

Ava really didn't want to go there since she was trying to block her problems out, but she shared with the girls the latest on her fairy tale marriage and the pictures Ryan received. Ava showed the girls the pictures of Sharon on her phone.

"She ought to be ashamed of herself," Lisa said.

"Damn, Ava! I've seen her at the office a couple of times when I go to see Carl. I'm going to ask him about this whore, she needs a beat down," Angela said, pissed by what she saw.

"Yep, that's the same lady I saw him with at the restaurant," Karen said.

"What are you going to do?" they all asked.

Turning her head to keep from crying, Ava told the girls she didn't know. Ava loved her husband and didn't believe in divorce, but she didn't know how much more she could take, either.

Angela held Ava as tears fell from her face. The girls all comforted her, while Ava felt like a fool staying with a man who was cheating on her.

"You know, what goes around comes around and karma is a bitch," Lisa said.

Ava shook it off and gathered herself together so she could eat her food.

"You know we need to go to that bitch's house and whip her ass," Karen said.

They all laughed because she was serious. Karen was crazy and they all knew it. The girls asked Ava about her health, talked about their kids, and going to Vegas before the year ends.

The girls finished their lunch, so that they could get back to work; but Ava sat there for a moment before heading out. The breeze was nice and Ava wasn't ready to go just yet.

---

Ava headed to the bank across town and talked to customer service about an account she had. Ava added Abbie and Jaxon's name on the account for the royalties of her books, which were automatically deposited into the account. They can only get money

*Love and War*

with an adult present, which would be Ava's mom, Elaine, or Alisse.

Ava also checked on other accounts that Ryan didn't know about and she planned on keeping things that way.

Ava didn't know what was going on, but she wasn't going to be a fool and let Ryan leave her and take the money she worked so hard for as well.

Ava left the bank when she noticed Angela calling.

"Hey, girl, you okay?" Angela asked.

"Yes, I'm good, why you ask?" Ava said.

"I know you and with all that's going on with Ryan, I just wanted to check back with you," Angela said.

"Thanks, I'll figure it all out," Ava said.

"Send me those pictures so I can ask Carl about the lady in the photographs," she said before hanging up.

"Will do," Ava said while she forwarded the pictures to Angela.

## *Wifey Material?*

$A$ngela was lying in bed when Carl came in to change. Carl looked exhausted from working late on a project that had to get done. Chrissy peeped in the room and smiled.

"Hi, dad," she said.

"Hi, Chrissy pooh. What you know good, baby girl?" Carl said to Chrissy.

"Nothing, just speaking since I haven't seen you all evening. I'm going back to my room now," Chrissy said walking down the hall dancing.

Carl smiled and said to Angela, "Our baby girl is growing up."

"Yes, she is, time really does fly," Angela said.

Carl walked over gave Angela a hug and kissed her. "How was your day?" he asked.

## Love and War

"Exhausting, I had patient after patient. I'm tired of looking at teeth," Angela said laughing. "I had lunch with the girls and guess what?" Angela said reaching for her phone.

Carl looked on, waiting for her to present whatever it was she was reaching for. Angela showed Carl the pictures Ava sent to her of Sharon.

His eyes got big, "What are these?" Carl asked while staring at the photos.

"That's Sharon, Ryan's side piece, the company whore! She had the audacity to send those photos to Ryan."

"So, I guess you got these from Ava?" he said looking at Angela.

"Yes, do you know anything about Ryan's affair with this lady? I mean I'm shocked. To flaunt your whore when you have a wife is so disrespectful on all levels," Angela said trying to make sense of it all.

Carl laughed at her while Angela got all bent out of shape. Carl said that he didn't know that much about the affair, but knows she's always at the office with Ryan. He said he heard she was sleeping with Ricky, also. Ryan hasn't said much to Carl because he figures Carl would tell Angela.

"So, this chick is just sleeping with everybody? What about you, Carl? You didn't tap that, did you?" Angela asked out of curiosity.

He looked at her quick. "What do you mean *what about me?*" he said rubbing her leg. "I got all the woman I need right here, no need to go out there and get caught up. Shit, woman, you crazy, you'll kill a bitch!" Carl said laughing while stripping to his boxers to go shower.

*Carl got that right, ain't nobody got time for that*, Angela thought. *I will fuck a bitch up about mine*. Angela was professional when she needed to be, but could turn into a beast when she needed to, as well.

Angela watched Carl go into the bathroom and heard the shower door close. She got up to go join him. Angela took off her gown and hung it behind the door then she opened the shower door quietly while Carl's back was turned and caressed him.

"Hey, hey sexy...I knew you was watching big daddy and wanted some of me," Carl said grinning.

"Is that right," Angela responded while kissing him.

---

Carl was at work trying to concentrate on the project he had to get done when he noticed Andrew. Andrew was a male gossip and knew everything about what was going on in the office. He was laughing while standing outside the hall.

"Andrew," Carl called him from inside his office.

"What's up, boss?" Andrew said, giving Carl some dap; a white boy who acted blacker than Carl.

"What you know good? You ain't got no work to do?" Carl asked him.

"Yes, I got work. I'm just coming from Ricky's office. I was reviewing a spreadsheet with him until Sharon knocked on the door, you know the big booty girl, who we got the contract with?" Andrew said.

"I thought she just came here once a week for a weekly meeting and signatures," Carl said trying to get the scoop.

"Yeah, she's supposed to, but since she's been seeing ole boy, she's practically here every day. Ricky told me to give him a minute; it was going to be awhile. He's still seeing her, too, I think," Andrew added.

Carl looked at Andrew and laughed. This boy sure knew a lot. Carl asked him how he knows. He said Ricky told him he was hitting that while Ryan is wining and dining her like a fool. Carl couldn't help but laugh. Carl told Andrew he had work to do and to close his door behind him.

Hours later Nicole, the receptionist, called and said Carl had a visitor. Nicole sent her up and it was his favorite girl, Angela.

"Babe, what a surprise," he said, standing up to greet his lovely wife.

"I knew you were working hard, so I brought you lunch."

"Hmm, I must have given it to you good last night for you to come all this way," he said winking at her.

"You did alright, buddy!" Angela said kissing Carl on the lips.

Angela stated she had to come that way to take Chrissy to her appointment and was headed back to work. Carl enjoyed seeing his wife every chance he got; she was hot.

Angela and Carl walked out of his office so that he could walk her downstairs. They came upon Ryan's office as Sharon was standing in this black fitting dress that revealed her sexy ass. Sharon's body was something serious, Carl had to admit. He had to do a double take and hope Angela didn't catch him looking.

Angela did a double take as well, stopped, knocked, and smiled at Ryan.

"Hi, Ryan," Angela said.

Sharon turned around and smiled. *Damn, she has nice legs, too*, Carl thought.

"Hi, Angela, good to see you," Ryan said

"Yeah, I bet. So, is this Sharon?" Angela asked, while Carl tried to wing her away.

"I beg your pardon," Sharon said caught off guard by Angela's question.

"You're Sharon, right? I noticed you from the photos I saw," Angela said.

*Love and War*

Oh shit, Carl had to get Angela out of there. He glanced down the hallway and saw Ricky, Andrew, and Brent walking their way.

"What photos?" Sharon asked, while Ryan stood there wondering the same thing.

"These," as Angela pulled out her cell phone and showed Sharon the disgraceful photos she took that were intended for Ryan as Ryan looked on.

"Yes, you're sleeping with my best friend's husband and you should be ashamed of yourself." Angela said. "This shit ain't classy, and you know he's married, sending a married man naked photos of your ass!"

"You have some nerve! How did you get those? Let me guess. Ava? Did Ryan tell you he was divorcing her?" Sharon said like Ryan was already her man.

Carl had to grab Angela because she was about to let Miss Thing have it.

"Sharon, let me explain…Carl please take Angela and leave," Ryan said.

Everyone was standing around Ryan's office watching while Ricky laughed. Carl grabbed Angela, trying to get her to leave.

"Divorce, Ryan? Really? For this whore? Ava deserves better than this shit!" Angela said before leaving.

"Angela, please leave now!" Ryan hollered.

They left as Carl heard Ryan's door slam and everyone was in shock at what they just heard. Carl heard Ricky say, "Sharon wasn't no good. She'll bend over for anyone," as everyone laughed. Carl watched Angela, who was pissed, giving looks at anyone who looked at her.

"Baby, calm down, this isn't your problem. Let Ava and Ryan figure this shit out on their own. I'll talk to him when I get back because I don't like this no more than you do," Carl said trying to ease her nerves.

Carl kissed Angela and watched her get in her car. He shook his head, and let out a deep breath...he headed back upstairs to find everyone whispering. Andrew said, "Tell Angela to forward us those photos of big booty Sharon." Carl looked at him and knocked on Ryan's door. Sharon was leaving as Carl walked in, then she turned her head his way and walked out.

"Ryan, man, I'm sorry about Angela's outburst. What's really going on man?" Carl asked.

"No problem. That's how women are. So I guess you saw the pictures, too, then?" Ryan asked.

"Yes, Ava was upset and sent them to Angela. They are best friends, what do you expect?"

Ryan went on to explain the incident at Jaxon's game and when Sharon sent the photos. He admitted he planned on leaving Ava because he wasn't in love with her anymore.

*Love and War*

Carl was shocked and in disbelief. "Man, Ava loves the ground you walk on! Is this about Sharon?" Carl asked. "You know she's still sleeping with Ricky? Everyone is talking about it," he said.

"Carl, I know all about that. With Sharon it's different. Besides that Ricky mess is in the past; you know he's a hater anyway so he's going to talk. A lot has been going on for awhile and I love Sharon," Ryan said, not sure if he's trying to convince himself or Carl.

Carl was not believing what he was seeing or hearing. He had to really look at Ryan. This wasn't the Ryan he knew. Ava was a good woman and even Carl knows she didn't deserve what Ryan was dishing out.

"What about Abbie and Jaxon?" Carl said

"I plan on talking to them soon. And Ava, too," he said.

"So I take it Ava doesn't know about the divorce you're planning?"

"Not yet."

Not wanting to hear any more of what Ryan had to say, Carl left his office. Carl couldn't believe that fool. *Damn, Sharon had a nice ass, but she wasn't all that*, Carl thought. *The grass isn't always greener on the other side and he will find that out sooner or later. Not sure if he's on something or just damn crazy.*

Carl got back to his office and called Angela to fill her in on his conversation with Ryan and she couldn't believe it, either.

73

Carl asked her not to say anything to Ava; he wanted Ava to fill Angela in when she learned of Ryan's plans or Angela would have to answer to Carl for opening her mouth!

## *Lies, Lies, Lies*

*R*yan woke up with a backache and headache from sleeping in the spare room. The bed he slept on wasn't as firm as the bed he and Ava shared. Ryan came home to a pissed off Ava who was in a rage after hearing from Angela about Sharon being at the office.

Ryan needed to ask Ava for a divorce, but needed to wait for a couple weeks to put things in place and talk to the kids. Abbie and Jaxon had no idea what was going on between them. Ava always kept the kids busy to avoid conflict.

Ryan looked at his cell phone and it read 4:30 a.m. and a missed call and voice message from Sharon. Ryan just left Sharon a couple hours ago, so he wasn't sure why she was calling; she knows to be patient with him. He laid there looking at the ceiling fantasizing about Sharon dancing for him and making love to him. Sharon's lips were all over his body, making Ryan feel good only to hear barking outside, which interrupted a session of his hands in his pants stroking himself.

Ryan quickly dialed Sharon, even though he knew she was sleeping; he just wanted to hear her voice.

"Hey, is everything okay?" Sharon asked in a deep sleepy voice.

"Yes, I just wanted to hear your voice. I was thinking about you."

"Is that so? I left you a voice message because you were also on my mind. This only means we are destined to be together," Sharon said.

"I know. I wanted you to talk dirty to me and put me to sleep," Ryan told Sharon who laughed at him.

"Babe, where are you?" she asked.

"I'm in the spare bedroom where I sleep, so start talking."

Sharon did what Ryan asked and he found a towel to put over his manhood because she had him going. Ryan was having phone sex with Sharon's words and his hands. Finally, Ryan felt himself drifting off to sleep and heard Sharon hang up.

"Kids, I need you to hurry and eat your breakfast!" Ava hollered. Abbie was taking her time trying to text and eat while Jaxon played around with Instagram with his phone. Ava had an

*Love and War*

important meeting that morning with her agent Elaine and didn't want to be late after dropping the kids off.

"Mom, tell Jaxon to stop taking pictures of me putting them on his Instagram page!" Abbie said with attitude.

Jaxon laughed, knowing he was aggravating his sister. "Jaxon, please stop. You know how your sister is," Ava said.

"Mom, look," Jaxon said, as Ava turned around and he took a picture from his phone.

"Boy, that's enough! It's too early, no more pictures," she said.

Moments later Ryan walked in looking for his breakfast. Confused, he asked, "Ava, where's my plate?"

"Kids, go get your bags and get in the car," Ava ordered.

Once they cleared the kitchen, Ryan was still standing there waiting on his food and coffee, but she only fixed breakfast for her and the kids.

"So, you didn't fix breakfast?" Ryan asked again.

"Yes," Ava said while he kept looking around. "For me and the kids. You can go to Sharon's and eat," she said grabbing her purse.

"Ava, let's not go there. I told you why she was at the office. Who you gonna believe me or Angela?" he said.

"It's surely not you, Ryan. Everything that comes out your mouth is a lie. I heard you talking to her this morning, you bastard," Ava said in a rage, throwing muffins at his ass.

Ryan couldn't say anything because she wasn't buying it. Ryan ducked as muffins went everywhere.

"Ava, babe, we need to talk," Ryan said.

Ava took her belongings and went to meet the kids in the car.

---

Ava met with her agent, who also had a representative from Lifeworld, a network that plays everyday life-filled movies and was interested in making her book, *If This World Was Mine*, an actual movie for their network. Ava was thrilled because never had she thought about turning any of her novels into an actual movie.

They all discussed the details, cost, actors, and everything else that involved production and filming. After the representative left, Ava's agent, Elaine, got up and did a happy dance; she was more excited than Ava.

"Ava, what do you think?" Elaine asked.

"Really, I'm still in shock," she said, smiling from ear to ear.

Elaine and Ava hugged. She suggested they celebrate, but it was way too early. Elaine was going to get with her attorney to go over the documents and contract.

*Love and War*

"A movie on Lifeworld?" Ava said getting the nerves to scream; what a dream!

Ava called her mom, Elaine, and Alisse to give them the news and they were screaming like crazy.

"Ma, can you believe it?" Ava said through the phone.

"Yes, girl, you're talented, so yes!" she said. Alisse cried, she was so happy for Ava. The two had been stuck together like glue since the day their Daddy left.

Ava said her goodbyes to Elaine, her agent, and headed to Angela's work. She drove in excitement and really wanted to call Ryan. This was a good day for her, but sad at the same time because she couldn't share it with her husband.

Ava waited on Angela to get done with her patient, who came out fifteen minutes later.

"Ava, is everything alright?" Angela asked.

"Yes, girl, I didn't know where to go. I got news," she said.

Angela pulled Ava into her office and she shouted, "My book is going to be a movie!"

"What!" Angela said jumping up and down.

Ava told her all about her meeting and wanted to share it with her. Ava would call Karen and Lisa as soon as she was done with Angela.

"Have you told you know who?" Angela asked concerned.

"No not sure if I plan to, although I want to," Ava said.

"You do what you feel, but the way I feel about Ryan is keep your money separate or hidden. I don't trust him. Sorry, but you're my girl," Angela said.

Ava understood exactly where she was coming from and getting at, and she told Angela that she was one step ahead of her. Angela smiled and said, "That's what I'm talking about."

Ava shared with Angela that, although she may be a fool dealing with Ryan's cheating, she has her reasons, first of which was she made a promise to God. "I'm not a fool when it comes to my assets, though," she said.

They both laughed as they hugged again before Ava went on her way.

Ava decided to stop by Ryan's office just for the hell of it. She left furious that morning so she knew he'd be shocked by her visit. Ava stopped and got bagels for everyone since she was in a good mood.

Nicole, the receptionist, sent her up as she spoke to everyone along the way. Ava announced that she brought bagels and pastries and was setting them in the break room. Some of the employees followed behind her.

"Thanks, Ava, for breakfast," Andrew said.

"Not a problem," Ava responded passing Ricky and Brent.

Ava went looking for Ryan who was coming out of his office.

"Baby, this is a surprise," Ryan said.

"I know I hated the way we ended things this morning and decided to bring bagels for everyone…and see you," Ava said really wanting to laugh.

"Bagels?"

"Yes, they're in the break room," she said.

"Ava, I'm sorry about this morning and anything else that I may have done," Ryan went on to say.

"Shhh…" Ava said walking towards him putting a finger to his lips. She grabbed Ryan by the hand and pulled him close to her giving him a long deep kiss and he kissed her back with all he had.

They heard someone standing at the door making a noise, "Excuse me."

It was Sharon, Ava saw her in the office she passed and that's why she kissed Ryan. "Yes, Sharon?" Ryan said with a stern look on his face.

"I have something for you to sign," Sharon said.

Sharon handed Ryan the piece of paper, he quickly signed it as she wanted to say something else. Ava smiled and spoke, "Is there's something else you want, Sharon? Perhaps my husband?"

"Yes, as a matter of fact, there is…Ryan when you're done with her, I need for you to call me," Sharon said turning to walk out the door.

"Will do, Sharon. When he's done with his wife, you can have the leftovers, bitch!" Ava said as she turned around and slammed the door in Sharon's face.

"Damn, girl, that door hurt *me*," Ava heard Andrew say.

"Shall we proceed, Ryan?" Ava said to him who was looking like he had just shitted in his pants.

## *Three Months Later*
## *Make up to Break up*

$A$va had been on a high since the release of her book and the filming of her movie. Everything was going rather smoothly, even with Ryan. Months had passed since Ava heard anything about Sharon, and Ryan seemed to be more attentive to her and the kids.

Ava was in Los Angeles for filming and brought the family along as a vacation. Ryan was so interested in Ava's life that he offered to help her direct. Although Ava said she had everything in place, she couldn't help wondering why the sudden change. Ryan seemed to be in love these days, more than ever before. Had he kicked Sharon to the curb or had she found a new man? Whatever it was, Ava hoped Sharon stayed away for good.

"Mom, can we go shopping?" Abbie asked.

"Maybe later after the set," Ava said.

Ryan pulled the kids away so that they could wrap up the scenes and took them inside the trailer. Ava watched them and was happy that he was spending more time with them.

Later they found themselves on Robertson Boulevard, then Rodeo Drive where all the celebrities go to shop. Abbie took pictures of everything; she even spotted Paris Hilton and got a picture with her. Ava went into Tiffany and Company and spotted a banging bangle only to look at the price; it was not so banging then. She found some nice bracelets engraved with *Our Friendship Lasts a Lifetime* and thought about the girls. The bracelets were a whopping $800 a piece. Ava spoke with a salesman and decided to order three of them. She also found Alisse something special, as well as her mom. The items will be shipped to her home in a couple weeks; the total bill was $4,000. With her blessings, Ava could afford to bless her friends.

Ryan grabbed Ava's hand as they walked, then they entered Saks Fifth Avenue; Ryan stated, "These prices are ridiculous."

Jaxon wanted to go to Niketown and Ava wanted to go in Neiman Marcus. Abbie followed her as Ryan followed Jaxon.

Ava loved to shop so she was in heaven.

"Mom, I got to have this Michael Kors bag. Mom! It's a crossbody…" Abbie begged.

Ava looked at her with those pretty eyes because she has created a monster, Abbie's taste was expensive. They looked around as Ava found the perfect pair of Christian Louboutin peep-

*Love and War*

toe pumps, Gucci sandals, a Celine orange handbag, and a Tory Burch handbag. Ava told Abbie she could get a couple more items, but they needed to hurry up to meet Ryan and Jaxon.

"Oh my," Ava said getting to the register.

Ava handed the cashier her credit card and couldn't believe what her receipt read. "Thanks, Mom," Abbie said, happy as she wanted to be, at least for the time being.

"Babe, how much did you spend?" Ryan asked.

"A couple thousand," Ava said.

"I know we got some money, but are we balling because our account is still the same?" Ryan said.

"This is some money I had put aside for this trip since we've been here filming, we're not balling, we are just shopping," Ava said trying to figure out what Ryan was getting at regarding her money.

They all had dinner at Barney's, the kid's choice. Ava was very sleepy. Getting up at the crack of dawn each morning was finally taking its toll on her. The kids enjoyed their vacation; they went to the beach, amusement park, sky diving, and lots of other activities. Even Ryan said he had a blast. As the night was ending, after they headed back to pack, the kids watched a movie while Ava and Ryan took a walk on the beach.

Ryan seemed like a different man than he was a couple months ago; this was the man Ava fell in love with. There were several people out enjoying the summer breeze.

"You know, Ava, this trip was nice. I admit I needed to get away," Ryan said.

"Yes, it was nice. We got the movie done and I'm pleased with it," Ava said.

"I'm so proud of you, you're doing big things," Ryan said.

Ryan took Ava's hand and led her to a tree; they sat, talked as she laid her head on his shoulder while he rubbed his hand through her hair. Ryan started cupping Ava's breast as he slipped his hand in her shorts and stated he wanted to make love to her. Ryan took off his clothes and laid them on the sand, then took Ava and made love to her slowly. Ava felt Ryan stroke and grind, taking his time. The pain Ava felt earlier subsided long enough for her to make love to her husband.

"Baby, you feel so good," Ryan said.

"You feel good, too. I missed you, Ryan," Ava responded while Ryan gave her all of him.

"I love the way you feel...I enjoy making love to you, Sharon...ahhhh, you feel so good," Ryan said without realizing he called her Sharon.

Ava quickly pushed Ryan off of her. Looking for her clothes in the dark, she scrambled. "What's wrong Ava?" Ryan asked.

"You have to ask, Ryan? All this time I thought you were changing! While you're making love to me, you're thinking about Sharon!" Ava hollered.

*Love and War*

She screamed, cursed, cried, and threw sand at Ryan.

"Ava, I didn't mean it! Really!" he said.

Ava had her clothes on and ran back to the room in tears. She couldn't believe Ryan; calling her another woman's name while he was inside of her. Ryan ran after Ava, realizing at the entrance that he had no pants on.

---

*A*rriving home from vacation and being on shoot, Ava was drained. She had not spoken to Ryan since he called her Sharon. All Ava thought about was how she could be so foolish and let this man continue to hurt her. *Was it love?* she thought. *Or was she that needy for a man?*

Ava contemplated calling Malcolm, the guy she meet at the restaurant, just to talk. Instead, she found herself texting him from the number on the card he had given her. Ava watched her phone waiting on a response when Ryan walked into the living room wanting to talk.

MSG: *Hi, you. It's finally nice to hear from you,* Malcolm replied.

Ignoring Ryan, Ava MSG back *I hesitated at first, but figured I better pay it forward since I owe you a drink*, she replied.

"Ava, are you listening to me?" Ryan asked. "I'm pouring my heart out trying to make us work and all you're doing is texting."

"Really, Ryan, what is up with you anyway? Your sudden interest in me…is Sharon seeing someone else?" Ava asked.

MSG *Is that your way of meeting up or should I ask would you like to have dinner with me* ☺ Malcolm replied with a smiley face.

"There is nothing between Sharon and I. I don't know what happened on that beach Ava, say something," Ryan pleaded.

MSG *I would love to…say 7:00 p.m. at Alinea* ☺

"Ryan, all is forgiven," Ava said walking off.

"Well how about dinner, then? Just me and you," Ryan said.

"Ryan, I already have plans. I'll make sure to fit you in my schedule," Ava said walking off laughing.

MSG *See you there!* Malcolm replied.

Out of all these years, Ava would not have thought she'd be having dinner with another man. Ryan left her with no choice.

Ryan followed her into the bedroom and all she wanted was to rest awhile before she met Malcolm. Ava lay across the bed. All of a sudden Ryan lay behind her, wrapping his arms around her, holding her tight. Ava wanted to move his arms, but thought, *What the hell; I'll just drift off this way…it'll keep him quiet for the moment.*

*Love and War*

Ava couldn't believe that, out of all the clothes she had, she still couldn't find anything to wear. Ava picked out an old knee-length dress with the back out, that went perfectly with the Christian Louboutin pumps she just purchased.

Ava hurried and got dressed looking at the clock since she was meeting Malcolm on the other side of town. Ava decided to wear her hair up, put on some lashes, sprayed Jimmy Choo perfume over her body, did a double take on her makeup, and did a spin for the mirror.

"Now, this was a red carpet look," she said, smiling at herself.

Abbie ran in the room with her camera and took a picture. She loved to copy Ava's style into her own when creating designs.

"Mom, you look good," Abbie said.

"Thanks, doll, kiss your brother for me and I'll see you guys in a bit," Ava said.

Ava grabbed her clutch to walk out, only to run into Ryan. "Damn, where you going with that dress on? It looks mighty short, your back is out, and exposing your breast," he said.

"Well, thanks Ryan, I'll see you later," Ava said turning around, "and please don't wait up!" she added leaving the house.

Nervous as a coo-coo bird, Ava arrived at Alinea, checked herself in the mirror, got out and handed the gentleman her keys. She walked in only to find Malcolm waiting for her.

"Hi, you," Malcolm said, hugging her. "You look really good. Is all this for me?"

"Well, thanks, and yes," Ava said, sweating like a mad woman.

"Table for two," Malcolm told the hostess. They followed the woman to a table in the back overlooking the river. Ava thought the table was perfect just in case someone spotted them. She had a few people come up wanting a picture when they recognized her face.

"I guess you're a celebrity and it's my honor to have dinner with you," Malcolm said.

Ava smiled and was speechless as this was her first date ever. She ordered a shot to calm her nerves as Malcolm laughed.

"What's so funny?" she asked looking at Malcolm.

He shook his head "A shot? You look like a margarita girl," he said.

Ava laughed and admitted she needed one to calm her nerves. He made her feel at ease when he admitted that he, too, was nervous, but told her to loosen up. The more Ava and Malcolm talked, the more she became attractive to him; his personality was warming.

*Love and War*

  They had a glass of Chardonnay while they waited on their dinner. Ava found out that Malcolm was an investment broker; he gave her a lot of tips on how to maneuver a couple stocks she was unsure about. Malcolm had a teenage son from a previous relationship with a woman with whom he shares custody. He also talked about where he lived, his likes and dislikes, and why he was still single.

  When it was her turn, Ava didn't know where to start.

  "So, tell me about your husband," Malcolm asked.

  Ava continued to eat her oysters and finally opened up about her life, kids, health issues, and success.

  "You mean to tell me your husband is cheating on you?" Malcolm asked.

  In shock he explained that some men have to pump up their egos when they feel like a woman is more successful than they are. Although Ryan makes a decent salary, Ava's salary was more due to her initiative - her books, speaking engagements and now, this movie. Ryan could feel even more threatened and his behavior may get worse.

  Ava never looked at it like that, but his statement kind of made sense. "You know, I never cheated on him, but here I am letting him cheat on me," she said.

  Malcolm took her hand. "Ava, I will never understand," he said.

Dinner was nice, it was good to get out and have a great time. Malcolm offered to cook Ava dinner whenever she was up for it; he knew she was married, so they toasted to a new beginning of simply being friends.

*Love and War*

## *Playing with Fire*

Carl seemed to be in a great mood, he walked into the office smiling. The last time Ryan talked to Carl, he was upset about Ryan's sudden divorce outburst. Since then the conversations had been awkward.

"Hey, man, how was your vacation? Angela told me about Ava's new movie, which will be shown around the world in a couple months," Carl said.

Ryan smiled and said, "It was great. L.A. was nice and the movie gave Ava a nice look."
Ryan walked over to his filing cabinet while Carl looked on breaking the space between them.

"Are you still planning to divorce Ava?" Carl asked concerned.

Ryan looked at Carl and asked, "What is it to you?"

"Ava is good people, man; we can get caught up in situations that we don't realize how good people are until they are gone," he said.

Carl apologized for meddling, but also updated Ryan on catching Ricky and Sharon in an awkward position when he went into his office. Ryan acted as though that didn't phase him, but he knew Sharon better than anybody and her playing Ricky was a way to get back at him for going on vacation with Ava.

Carl and Ryan chatted for a while until he was paged over the loud speaker that he had a phone call parked on line two.

Ryan tried to work, but was distracted with Ava getting in at 4:00 a.m. and Sharon ignoring him. Ryan stopped what he was doing and dialed Sharon. Ryan called several times and his calls went straight to voicemail. The last call he decided to leave a message.

*"H,i Sharon, I know you see me calling. I'm just sitting here thinking about you. I miss you; it's been four months already. I knew that waiting wouldn't be easy, but it will be finally worth it. Besides I got you something and want to give it to you, so please call me. I love you, Sharon. Call me back,"* Ryan said holding the phone before hanging up.

Ryan sat back in his chair and stared at the family photo of him, Ava, and the kids last year. They looked like the perfect family and he looked happy. He was not sure of the sudden change in himself; he just couldn't get back to being the man Ava

## Love and War

once knew. Although, he cared for her deeply, his heart was with Sharon.

He dialed Sharon again and left another message: *"Sharon, baby, if you don't call me back I swear I'm coming to your job with a tent and I'm camping out until you talk to me,"* Ryan said and hung up.

His phone rung…as he rushed to pick it up only to hear Carl's voice about getting together tonight at his and Angela's house. Although Ryan wasn't in the mood, he said yes and hung up. Moments later, Ava text him about going to a get together at Angela's this evening while her mom watched the kids. Ryan replied, *sure*, only to turn his attention back to Sharon.

Ever since that day Ava came to the office with bagels and Sharon saw them kissing, his life has gone downhill. When Sharon found out about the family vacation, she stopped speaking to him. Ryan couldn't focus; enough was enough! It was now lunch time and the office was empty minus a few, so he grabbed his keys and headed for the door.

Ryan walked out only to find Sharon walking towards him. "Ryan, we need to talk," Sharon said.

Ryan walked back in his office and closed and locked the door after Sharon came in. Sharon stood as he embraced her in his arms, rubbing her face. "I missed you, you know that?" Ryan said. Sharon smiled, but didn't respond.

"Did you get my messages?" Ryan asked.

Sharon finally cracked a smile, "Yes, all 150 of them," she said.

"Baby, we let months get in the way of us, if we're going to be together we have to stick it out while being patient," he said.

"Ryan, it's hard and Ava is making it her duty to keep you," she said.

Ryan took Sharon's hand and told her not to worry about a thing. He then kissed her long and hard only to come up for air.

Knowing that everyone had pretty much gone to lunch, he undressed Sharon down to her purple thong, her breasts stood at attention while he struggled to get his clothes off.

"Sharon, sit in the chair."

She did as she was told. Ryan spread her legs apart, putting one leg on the edge of the desk and the other one over his shoulder. Ryan went in like he'd been waiting on this meal all day. He sucked all Sharon's juices, licked the outside of her minora while he spread her lips apart and played with her clitoris.

Sharon begged Ryan to stop and enter her. He came up and cupped both breasts and sucked them one by one. He entered her...pulled out...entered...teasing her until she begged for it. "Ryan, I don't want you to stop, fuck me, please," she said.

Ryan liked it when she talked dirty to him.

"That's right, daddy, fuck me harder."

*Love and War*

It felt so good getting his dick wet inside of Sharon; she had some good pussy and knew it, too. Ryan could tell how she threw it back. "Whose pussy is this?" he asked her.

"It's your pussy, baby," she said as she bounced her titties in the chair. Ryan watched the expressions she made and loved them; she was in her zone.

"I'm about to cum," she said as he went deeper...deeper making her cum. With sweat running down her face, Ryan made her turn over in the chair...ass out!

"Bring that dick here so I can kiss it."

Ryan stood in front of Sharon while she sat in the chair as she took daddy's long stroke in her warm mouth.

"Damn, you have a huge dick," she said.

"And it's all yours," he said, waiting to cum in her mouth.

Sharon knew how to make a man go crazy, her tongue was a weapon used to make him bust quick. She slobbered, slurped, and drooled all over him. Ryan felt himself about to explode as she tried to pull out. He put his hand on her head...pushing it...keeping her latched on...1...2...3..."Ahhhh," Ryan let out a sigh of relief. Sharon did that.

Hearing voices and people coming back from lunch, he quickly spread both of her ass cheeks while grinding in her slowly; then he sped up the process. He pulled out and licked her anus. Ryan had his whole face in her ass, which made her even wetter.

He entered her again, slapping his balls against her ass cheeks. "You bastard, I don't feel you," she said.

"Well, you gonna feel this," Ryan said fucking her harder while sticking one finger in her anus. Sharon didn't like anal sex, but Ava loved it and he was going to make Sharon love it as well if she planned on being with him. After five more minutes of pumping, they both came together, as he slumped against the trash can.

"Wow, that was a workout, Ryan!" Sharon said.

"Yep, tell me about it," he said, catching his breath to speak.

They managed to gather their clothes, clean themselves up, and get dressed. Ryan had to Lysol the office down it smelled just like ass...and mo ass! He kissed Sharon and thanked her for coming by and blessing him with her talent.

"It was my pleasure," she said smiling.

"Oh, I got something for you," as he remembered the diamond earrings he bought in LA.

Sharon opened the box and was amazed with the diamond-studded hoops he bought her. "Thanks, babe, these are gorgeous!" She took off the ones she was wearing, replacing them with the ones Ryan gave her. By the look on her face, he could tell she was thrilled.

*Love and War*

"Can you come by later?" Sharon asked. Remembering the gathering, he told Sharon Jaxon had a game, but maybe tomorrow. They said their goodbyes, then Sharon left.

Ryan was finally able to concentrate now that all was forgiven by Sharon.

---

Ava was getting dressed when Ryan got home, she had already laid out his clothes for the evening. All he had to do was shower.

One thing about Ava and Ryan they always coordinate their clothes when they stepped out together. Ryan watched her as he dressed wondering how she was going to react to him asking for a divorce. Would she let him go? Try to hold on? Go crazy? Something he couldn't answer, but he prepared himself for the worse.

They got to Carl and Angela's house and were greeted with wine and hors d'oeuvres. It was a small gathering, but nice; Karen and her new man were there, and Lisa and her new man as well. Alisse and her fiancée, Justin, Angela's sister, and a few of Angela's co-workers from her office.

"Don't you two look lovely," Angela said greeting them not looking at Ryan.

Ryan excused himself and headed toward Carl and Justin, while the fellas talked basketball and baseball. Ryan noticed Angela and Carl went way out with caterers and live music. With Angela's money, she and Carl had a nice, big, beautiful home.

"What's up big boi?" Ryan said to Justin giving him a bear hug. Justin and Alisse were about to tie the knot, although Alisse and Ava's taste in men were different, Justin was cool and well off.

They all walked over to the bar and he noticed Ava and the girls chopping it up. Getting bored, Ryan excuse himself to the restroom to text Sharon.

MSG: *Hey, babe, how's your evening?*

Minutes later...MSG: *It's great; Tiffany and I just came back from dinner. Now I'm about to exhale*, Sharon replied.

"Ryan," he heard Ava call out. Ryan hurried and texted Sharon back. MSG: *I love you, future Mrs. Decree!*

Ryan walked out of the restroom. "We're ready to eat," Ava said. He followed her out as they all went out on the patio. Ava introduced Ryan to Lisa's friend, Jonathan, and Karen's new man, Chris, who was all hugged up with Karen. They sat at a huge table filled with seafood, steak, kabobs, steamed vegetables, salad, and rolls.

Ryan noticed Ava texting and wondered who she could be talking to besides the kids. He tried to glance, but she turned her back full force and smiled after hitting send. Angela was giving a speech and toast about expanding her dental practice adding more

## Love and War

dentists while introducing her newest Hygienist at the table. Everyone was excited and thrilled for Angela and her expansion.

"I'm so proud of you!" Ava said, teary eyed.

They all toasted to Angela's news as Karen stood up and announced she was pregnant. "Get outta here!" Lisa said running over to hug her friend.

"What!" Angela yelled in excitement. "I'm gonna be an auntie..."Ava, Angela, and Lisa sang as they hugged on Karen and congratulated her boyfriend, Chris. Ryan couldn't remember his name, so he figured he was the daddy. Ryan looked at the other guests who were waiting for the excitement to end so they could eat.

"With all this great news, let's eat!" Carl hollered.

The food was great, the weather was nice, and everyone seemed to be enjoying themselves. The drunker everyone got, the crazier the conversations got. The conversation turned from monogamy to infidelity, then sex. Ryan remained tight lipped, not trying to say anything out of the way.

"So, Ryan what do you think about monogamy?" Karen asked as everyone turned their attention to him, including Ava.

Ryan cleared his throat, knowing she did that on purpose, while he tried to find the right answer to the question. "Monogamy is great when you have that mate you connect with and plan to spend the rest of your life with," he managed to say.

"What about sexual partners outside of the relationship?" Angela asked adding fuel to the fire.

"I want to hear this," Ava said, while everyone else was curious as to why his wife made that comment.

"Like I said, if you and your mate connect, a person won't have a need for multiple sexual partners," Ryan said breaking out a sweat.

Everyone started talking as Ava blurted, "Oh, I get it now; we don't connect Ryan. That's the reason you have multiple sex partners and call me by her name during sex, right?" Ava said standing up to toast to "multiple sex partners."

Ryan was embarrassed as hell, Ava yelled sounding drunk, "Ryan fucks Sharon y'all!" She then threw her napkin on the table and stormed inside as Alisse and Angela ran in behind her.

"I'm sorry, man," Carl managed to say as the other guests said their goodbyes and dismissed themselves. Angela's sister stayed behind to help clean up, as Karen and Lisa went inside to check on Ava.

"Fellas, I'm sorry for my wife's outburst," Ryan said apologizing while they tried to figure out what was going on.

After minutes of sitting, Ryan went inside to tell Ava it was time to go, he was tired of this bullshit.

"Ladies, I need to take Ava home," Ryan said.

Ava's eyes were red from crying; she gathered her things and told the girls good night.

*Love and War*

"That's a good woman you have, Ryan, all the ass in the world won't compare to what you have at home. Cherish her while you have her," Lisa said, as Ryan looked back only to turn around not responding.

Lisa thought she knew every damn thing and Angela was one of those women that liked control, a reason why Carl was scared to make a damn move. *Some black girls were a trip*, Ryan thought.

He drove them home in silent as Ava's blonde hair blew from the breeze. Ava's white skin looked pale, she usually went to the tanning salon, but it looked like she had not been in months. Ryan still embarrassed by Ava's actions only confirmed that he needed to move forward with the divorce before it got any worse.

*Bianca Harrison*

## *For Better or for Worse*

$A$ couple of weeks had passed since the incident at Angela's. The girls were coming over for brunch as Ava hurried to get back to the house with the food. Abbie ran out to help her while Jaxon played basketball with his friends.

The kids had been Ava's rock because she and Ryan rarely talk. He was spending more time elsewhere than at home, which she figured meant he went over to Sharon's. He wined and dined her and her daughter more than his own kids, which they also noticed.

"Mom, why do you have all this food?" Abbie asked as Jaxon came running down the street.

That *boy can smell food a mile away*, she thought. "Jaxon, slow down before you hurt yourself!"

"Mom, what you got? I'm hungry again!" Jaxon said, looking through the bags. "Boy, you better go wash your hands!" she scolded.

*Love and War*

"Abbie, put these subs on that tray," Ava watched Ryan walk into the room about to head out as usual.

"Dad, where are you going? Can we go to the movies later?" Jaxon asked Ryan.

"Maybe, son, depending on what time I get back," Ryan said.

"So that means no!" Jaxon said grabbing a sub, juice, and chips heading for the table. Abbie looked at Ava and smiled. "What?" Ava said.

"Nothing, Ma, I admire you, you know that," she said as Ava gave her a hug.

"Jaxon, baby, if you want to go to the movies later, I'll drop you and your friends off," Ava yelled.

Boy, he ran back in the room so quickly, "Really? Did you want to go, too, Abbie?"

"Sure, I want to see that new movie *Dark in the Fiery*. I'm going to call Kelly," Abbie said. Ava managed to pour the juice into the juice bowl and dip into a crystal bowl.

"So, I take it you don't want me to spend time with my son?" Ryan said not realizing Jaxon was still standing in the corner.

"Ryan, no offense, but you haven't been a father to these kids lately. You're too busy trying to take care of someone else's child. Yeah, word gets around quick. By the way, how *is* little Tiffany?" Ava asked him as he looked like dumb and dumber.

105

"Woman, what are you talking about?" Ryan said as the doorbell rang.

"Mom, it's Auntie Lisa," Jaxon yelled. Ryan was so pissed he grabbed his keys and walked out, which was nothing new these days. Ava swore she needed to figure out what to do before she lost her mind.

The rest of the girls came in moments after Lisa, including Chrissy. Karen had a glow about herself and Ava was so....so happy for her.

"What's up, mommy to be?" Angela joked rubbing her belly.

"Girl, stop it!" Karen said playfully. They all went around the table putting food on their plates and headed out to the sit under the gazebo.

"Girl, this food is delicious!" Karen said.

"Mom," Jaxon yelled from the back deck. "Dad just called and said he's taking us to the movies later," and went back in.

"That's nice of Ryan," Angela said.

"Yeah," Ava said updating the ladies on the entire situation since Angela's gathering.

"No offense, Ava, cause you're my girl, but a black woman would have left his ass a long time ago!" Lisa said with a mouth full of food.

*Love and War*

Looking in Karen's direction, Ava asked, "Karen, you've dated a black man before, what you think of him compared to the others you've dated?"

Karen explained that it was no difference, only in color; but respect was one thing. If a man didn't respect you, he definitely didn't love you enough. Ava really felt small after her statement. What has she done for Ryan to treat her the way he did?

"Ava, it's a control issue," Karen stressed.

Ava quickly changed the subject and talked about Malcolm. The girls were all in shock that they'd been going out.

"Ava, my girl, is going back to the cream," Angela said as everyone laughed.

Ava stressed that their friendship was nothing more, but it was great to have someone to talk to.

"He understands me and it's good to know I still look good for someone," Ava said smiling from ear to ear. Lisa got up, did her l'il dance called the squirrel and that's exactly what it looked like.

"We need music, Abbieee and Chriss-sssyyyy," Lisa yelled dragging out the girl's name.

"Shhhh, girl, you're not in the hood!" Ava snapped getting her to shut up, only she laughed like it was funny.

"Yes, Auntie Lisa," Abbie said over the deck as Chrissy followed.

"I need you to bring a radio down and play some of y'all music," Lisa said.

Moments later they found themselves doing the cupid shuffle, the wobble and a new dance rave called the nae nae. Abbie and Chrissy laughed at Lisa who was giving them a show. To know Lisa was to love her. Abbie and Chrissy went back inside after snapping a couple of photos probably to put on Instagram calling them old.

Ava knew that ring tone as she heard her phone ringing, but couldn't find it; she located it under some napkins.

"Lisa, turn the music down, it's Malcolm!"

Ava answered followed by, "Hi, Malcolmmmm," the girls said in harmony.

Malcolm was on Face Time so it was nice seeing him. He smiled and asked about Ava's evening, of course she was free.

"I'm taking you dancing, diva," Malcolm said.

"Dancing?"

"What's the problem? You can't shake?" Malcolm said as Ava fell over laughing.

"Somebody got soul!" Angela hollered.

Ava promised to meet him at his place so they could have some fun. She was excited like a school girl out of school on a snow day. Ava hung up only to hear Karen say, "Go get'em, girl!" Lisa was still trying to dance with two left feet and they say white girls can't dance.

*Love and War*

They all calmed down and finished talking; they had so much to catch up on until Ava saw in her hyperopic vision that Ryan was making his way to the gazebo. All the ladies started snickering, making eye contact with one another, and it got quiet when he finally made his way over.

"Ladies, are you enjoying this lovely day?" Ryan asked nervously.

"Ryan, what do you need?" Ava asked.

"Food, dear, is there any left?" he asked.

Angela shook her head in disbelief. "Whatever is left you may have," Ava said trying to get him to leave. Hell she thought he was gone, what did he come back for?

After Ryan disappeared, the girls helped clean up. Ava looked at the time and thought she had a few hours before seeing Malcolm.

"Girl, that husband of yours is a trip! I think he's going through a phase," Angela said.

"More like a mid-life crisis!" Lisa chimed in.

"You would think after all these years you pretty much know your mate, clearly that's not true," Ava said.

"Awe, Av, it will be okay," Karen said, as they all hugged each other.

It felt good talking to the girls. Ava felt like the more time she spent with Malcolm the less she thought about Ryan. Ava had to admit she loved her husband and this thing with Malcolm was strictly fun. Ava didn't want Malcolm to get caught in the crossfire with her and Ryan; he was too good for that.

---

Ava pulled out the garage only to forget her purse. She pulled back in as Jaxon was coming out with it, "Thanks, son!"

Ava exited out of the subdivision only to get behind a slow driver; she bypassed the guy trying to get on the expressway and hit Hamilton Mill. Malcolm stayed on the other side of town, a ways off, in a very expensive condo. Glancing at the clock, Ava saw she was right on time.

Ava got out her car wearing a fitted lace zigzag dress, flared, which was made for dancing, and a pair of black lace Dolce and Gabbana peep toe pumps. Ava loved to dress up; it made her feel good, sort of like a princess. Ava looked up and saw Malcolm coming down.

"Don't you look stunning," he said smiling like he was going to get some.

"You clean up rather well yourself," Ava said, looking at him in his Armani dress pants, pleated shirt, and Jordan's. He noticed Ava eyeing the shoes, "What? You don't like my kicks with my attire?" he asked.

Ava smiled, "They cool."

*Love and War*

"Beautiful, I wouldn't leave you hanging. I got my dancing shoes in the car. I have to look good standing next to you," Malcolm said making Ava blush.

Malcolm was Ava's knight in shining armor, he was a stress reliever. Just to kick it and talk was good enough without having to be physical.

"So, where are you taking me?" Ava asked.

"To LaParellu, where we can dine and have a good ole time," he said. "For a white boy, I got moves, girl, I want to see you do the Rumba…" Malcolm said.

Ava looked at him and burst out laughing, "You want me to do what?"

Malcolm drove to the next city, "I hope you don't have a curfew, this is going to be a long night. We gonna do a l'il Salsa, Cha-Cha-Cha, a l'il Hip-Hop, only to close out with the Hustle."

LaParellu seemed to be the spot; it was a nice atmosphere with a mature crowd. Dancing was everywhere; the food selection was amazing, as was the wine and alcohol selection. *A nice place for a first date*, Ava thought.

"So, what do you think so far?" Malcolm asked.

"This place is amazing! I never heard of it."

"One of my partners suggested this spot and I've heard nice things about it. I've always wanted to come, but needed the right woman to bring," he said winking at her.

Ava gave him the side eye and a sly smile, not showing him the effect he was having on her.

They placed their orders and headed for the dance floor. They did the rump shaker off of Latin music, only to end up doing the tango. Boy was Ava embarrassed, talk about Lisa, she had two bad feet. Malcolm laughed his ass off, "You think this is funny?" Ava asked, having the time of her life.

"No...no you're good, this is all for fun, but follow me," he said leading the way.

Ava caught on pretty quickly, enough to not make a fool out of herself. The waiter tapped them on the shoulder to let them know their dinner was ready. Ava ordered a glass of Merlot and Malcolm ordered Chianti, which went well with his pasta. The night was going rather smoothly.

*Malcolm, loosen up*, Ava thought. She could tell he had something on his mind.

"Talk to me," she said.

"About?"

"Whatever is on your mind."

Malcolm smiled sheepishly, "I like you, you know, but your world is so complicated; why do you put up with him?" he said, referring to Ryan.

"I know and honestly, I don't know. Malcolm, I like what we have because it's not complicated, more like a breath of fresh air," Ava said.

*Love and War*

He looked at her not knowing what he was going to say, "You're worth waiting for."

Ava couldn't believe what he just said. She wanted so desperately to make love to Malcolm, but couldn't bring herself to it. Ava had a vow to Ryan, even though he broke his vow to her; her commitment to God was all she could think about…would God forgive her? Call Ava a sinner? She wasn't sure, but was too scared to find out.

Ava took Malcolm's hand, "I adore you, you just don't know how you've made me feel these last couple of weeks. Thank you," she said.

They laughed, talked, and danced to what seemed like the wee hours of the night. They left around 2:00 a.m. only to find themselves by the river talking and acting silly. They then drove all the way back to Malcolm's condo where Ava went in and used the restroom before leaving.

His place was decked out. Ava noticed a Scarface picture on the wall, she turned to ask...

"A broker gave me that as a house warming gift, trying to be funny, but I like it," Malcolm said before she could get her question out. "Would you like some coffee before you leave?"

"No, thanks. I'll never make it home," Ava said walking to take a look out his balcony.

It felt good out as Malcolm came behind her and squeezed her tight. Ava felt some type of way as she turned around towards him.

"Shhh, whenever you're ready. Right now, let's just enjoy this moment," Malcolm said pulling Ava tight as she put her head on his shoulder.

Ava lifted her head up after a brief second and said, "Thank you." She found her way to his lips and kissed him passionately good night.

## Six Months Later
## Damned If You Do, Damned If You Don't

Ava was at her desk writing when she heard someone come in; she went to look and saw that it was Ryan. Ryan and Ava's marriage was rocky; they haven't touched each other in months although they still slept together from time to time. Ava tried her best to make things work, but Ryan seemed distant and pushed her away every time.

 Ava went back to writing in her journal, thinking about putting it all together for a book. Ava had a couple more book signings this month before she decided to relax.

 The phone rang and it was the practitioner calling in a prescription for the cramps and heavy periods she was experiencing. Ryan peeped inside the office, "Do you have a moment?"

 "Sure," Ava stopped what she was doing as Ryan came in and sat down in front of the desk.

"I wanted to talk about our finances, especially our account," he said.

Curious because there was nothing wrong with the accounts to her knowledge, Ava asked him to go ahead.

"I know we both have separate accounts plus our main account, but what about the money from the sale of the books and this Lifeworld movie deal?" Ryan asked nonchalantly.

Shocked at what he just asked, Ava had to clear her throat, "Ryan, what about the sale of the books? My money is my money and what's yours is yours," Ava said.

Not liking what Ava just said, Ryan said in a brushed tone, "I agree, but when you make more, that portion should go into our joint account."

"Says who?" Ava yelled, getting heated. "If I recall, we both signed a prenup that you put together and were so hell bent about when we got married. And now that I've made a name for myself and bring in more than you do, you think you gonna take my money to spend on your cheap broad? I don't think so!"

Ava got up from her desk, "I suggest you read your prenup, this conversation is over!" Ava said and walked off, as Ryan was right on her heels.

Ryan grabbed Ava's arm, "Don't you dare walk away from me, woman!"

"Ryan, what the hell has gotten into you?" Ava looked at him in pain as tears formed.

*Love and War*

"This is not the man I once knew; you get new pussy and take it out on me?" Ava removed his hands off of her and headed upstairs.

"Ava, baby, I'm sorry. I didn't mean to grab your arm like that," Ryan yelled up the stairway.

Ava went to shower so that she could feel some relief. She stood there, wanting to cry, but not a single tear came out. Her cramps were getting worse and all she wanted to do was lay down.

Ava got out of the shower and put on some comfy clothes, only to find Ryan sitting on the bed with some lilies he dug up from the yard. Ava thought, *This man has to be bipolar.* He made her feel so ridiculous that she walked pass him straight to her drawer. Ryan leapt from the bed coming up behind her only to apologize again.

Ava pushed the lilies away, only for him to say, "You like?"

"No, Ryan only in the yard," she continued to ignore him. She went to her phone and texted Malcolm back so that she could get out of the house.

MSG: *See you in an hour, lunch on me! SoHo that is.*

MSG: *I'll be there :)*

Ava powdered her face, brushed her hair back, and looked for a comfy pair of flats. Ava didn't feel cute, but still looked good to the mirror.

"You're just going to ignore me and leave?" he said.

"Yes, Ryan, I have to be somewhere."

"You look good, but you always do," he said.

Ava looked at him because he hasn't said that to her in forever. She was not sure what his motive was behind the comment, but she'd play along.

"Thanks, Ryan, I haven't heard those words from you in a very long time," Ava smiled and kept it moving.

---

Ava left the house annoyed, thinking the man she married all these years could be so ruthless and ask about her money. She has never asked about his money when he made more money than she did before she started writing, Ava wondered what was he up to and with whom. She'll be damned if he takes her money and uses it on Sharon! Just the thought alone made her sick.

Driving along Beacon Ridge Interstate, Ava saw a couple and their kids traveling with luggage and they seemed so happy. Ava wished that she could get back to that place with Ryan, it seem like he had changed overnight and the man he became, she didn't like.

Ava finally arrived at SoHo and was looking for Malcolm when he crept up behind her.

*Love and War*

"Hey, beautiful," Malcolm whispered in her ear. All the tense thoughts she had about Ryan turned into a smile and she credited Malcolm for that. Ava turned around and hugged him.

"Come, follow me," Malcolm said taking her hand.

Ava followed him to a secluded area that seemed to be just for him and her. "Wow, these are nice," Ava said taking the roses Malcolm handed her. He pulled out her chair as she seated herself, then motioned for the waiter.

Ava watched him tell the waiter to bring certain foods to the table and wondered why. Malcolm sat down with a smile.

"What's up with the special food order?" she asked him.

"I ordered your favorites, which have become my favorites also: frilled salmon Thai, iron steak, crab cakes, calamari, butternut squash, steamed rice, shall I say more?" Malcolm said. "Besides, the owner is my brother," Malcolm said smiling.

"Get out of here!" Ava said. "I guess that explains why you get special treatment."

Malcolm shook his head. Ava glanced around the restaurant; there was not a familiar face in sight. Not realizing she had zoned out, Malcolm stared at Ava waiting for her to come back to earth. "My bad, Malcolm, I was admiring the atmosphere."

"What's on your mind?" he asked.

Not wanting to get into it, Ava ended up spilling her guts to Malcolm. She explained what happened and went on about not understanding why Ryan was so concerned about her money.

Being an investment broker, Malcolm advised Ava to move her money to an offshore account, maybe in her kids' names, that way the money couldn't be tracked by him or the IRS. If something happened, she could add Alisse's name to the account.

Malcolm was very knowledgeable in international diversification, Swiss accounts, seizing, foreign regulations, all of which were new to her. He suggested that Ava keep a couple thousand, not too much, in her account for her royalties and all other assets to throw anyone looking into her account off the scent.

"Thanks, Malcolm, that was a lot of valuable information," Ava said.

"What do you think he's planning?" Malcolm asked.

"I'm not sure, maybe trying to take my money and leave me," she said laughing, knowing it may be true.

"Ava why did you marry him, a black man at that?" Malcolm asked. "No offense, I'm just curious, Ava; your background is totally different from his, that's all."

Ava looked at Malcolm trying to find the right words. "Well, Malcolm, it was not about the color. It was about the man I fell in love with. Ryan is no different than any other man. You all have the same thing, color isn't a factor to me," Ava said noticing Malcolm's reaction. "Besides I'm sitting here with you, which means I like cream as well," she said smiling at him.

Just in time the waiter brought all the items Malcolm ordered, which looked divine. A gentleman walked out and

*Love and War*

introduced himself as Mark, when he started talking about how special Ava was to Malcolm, she instantly knew that was his brother. They shook hands; Ava looks over at Malcolm giving Mark the thumbs up as if he did a good job preparing a nice setting for them.

"Please, if you want anything else, just let your waiter know as it's on the house," Mark said. He left them alone while greeting other customers seated in the restaurant.

The waiter brought out a bottle of Chardonnay and poured two glasses, which went well with all the food.

The food was amazing; Ava loved all the vegetables especially the squash and asparagus. "So, how is it?" Malcolm asked.

Ava gave it two thumbs up, "Excellent!"

"Don't you have to get back to work?" she asked Malcolm.

"Not until I'm done having lunch with the beautiful lady seated in front of me; besides I'm the boss," Malcolm said.

It was good to see how successful Malcolm and his brother, Mark, were; his background was very bleak. He had been moved around from foster care to foster care, only having his brother to depend on.

Ava's concern with Malcolm was waiting on her; at this point Ava had no idea where her life was heading, so she didn't want him to miss out on happiness even if it was with someone else.

*Bianca Harrison*

## *The Grass on the Other Side*

**R**yan loved every bit of his weekend with Sharon and Tiffany.

Ava was in Vegas for a book signing event and took the girls along for a weekend getaway.

Ryan took the kids over to his mom and made sure she kept them busy doing whatever they liked. Ryan's mom thought he was out of town on business, but little did she know he was spending the weekend with Sharon, the other woman in his life.

Ryan and Sharon were in the kitchen baking brownies and cookies while throwing dough at each other.

"So, Ryan you're planning on telling Ava next week right?" Sharon asked to assure what Ryan told her.

"Yes, I do, I've dragged it out long enough," he said.

"What about the money? You think she's going to give you half from all those books and the movie deal? You are entitled to it, you know," Sharon said.

"I'm not sure, but plan on fighting her for it if I have to. We both signed a prenup early on," he said.

"A prenup! Ryan, you should be able to fight her on that," Sharon said.

"Yeah, but I'm the one who demanded we sign one when we got married." Sharon walked over to the sink not saying a word. "What is it? You should be happy," he said.

"Ryan, what did you see in Ava? I mean, is it different dating a white woman verses a black woman? I never dated outside of my race and wouldn't know," Sharon asked waiting for a response.

"Are the brownies done yet?" Tiffany asked running into the kitchen.

"Not yet, baby, go play," Sharon said scooting Tiffany out the kitchen.

Ryan pulled Sharon to the empty chair in the kitchen and explained to her the difference between her and Ava. "Sharon, honestly love has no color, so when you see a black man with a white woman don't think negative, people date outside their race everyday," he said.

He then looked at her pull her hair back, "I loved Ava for Ava, don't get it twisted. Ava ain't no trailer park trash; she's high maintenance. And I love Sharon for Sharon. What you give me no longer exists between Ava and me," he said trying to reassure her thoughts.

Sharon smiled like she won the Nobel Peace Prize. She got up and checked on the brownies and cookies as Ryan watched her and thought about how good she'll be with Jaxon and Abbie.

Ryan's phone started buzzing and saw it was Carl calling. Not wanting to talk, he let the voicemail pick it up.

Tiffany ran back in with a friend looking for the baked goods as Sharon was putting them on a plate. "Be careful, kids, those are hot; get a paper plate first," she said.

Ryan listened to the message from Carl: "What's up, man? I was just calling and checking on ya since the ladies are away. Wanted to see if you wanted to get together with me and the fellas later and hit up a bar. Holla back and let me know the move. Peace."

Ryan deleted the message, "What is it?" Sharon asked.

"Nothing just a message from Carl wanting to get together later," he said.

Sharon shrugged her shoulders only to walk over and rub Ryan's head. "This has been a great weekend," Sharon said nibbling on his ear.

He smiled, hearing his phone go off again only this time it was Jaxon. "Hey son, what's going on?" Ryan asked.

"Dad, I'm ready to come home," Jaxon said.

"I'll pick you and your sister up tomorrow, I'm out of town," Ryan said lying to his son.

*Love and War*

"Out of town? Mom said you should be at home watching us, instead you dropped us off. I'm ready to come home, Dad. It's boring here," Jaxon whined.

*That damn Ava*, Ryan thought. "Jaxon, don't listen to your Mom. Maybe she forgot I was leaving for the weekend, I'll come get you first thing in the morning."

Click, click. Jaxon hung up. Ryan looked at the phone and heard the dial tone. "I know he just didn't hang up on me," he said still holding the phone.

Sitting there not knowing what to do, he heard Sharon tell Tiffany to stay over at her friend's house for awhile and walked back into the kitchen.

"Why is that bitch trying to ruin our weekend, Ryan?"

Snapping out of a daze, "Huh? Who? You mean Ava?"

"Yes, now she's using the kids against you. I want to see her face when you throw those divorce papers at her," Sharon said getting all hung up over Jaxon's phone call.

"Baby, calm down," he said grabbing her by the waist.

Ryan kissed Sharon so she would hush, got up from his chair while taking off his clothes, leaving his cotton boxers and socks on, just in case Tiffany ran back in.

Sharon looked at him. "What are you doing, Ryan?" Sharon protested while looking at his dick through his boxers.

"Make sure the door is locked, I heard you tell Tiffany to stay at her friend's house for awhile. Is this what you want?" Ryan

125

said pulling down his boxers. While his dick stood at attention, he started moving his hand up and down his shaft letting out precum.

Ryan headed to the bedroom; he wasn't worried about Sharon. He knew she would be behind him in seconds. He lay on the bed with his dick straight up in the air stroking it up and down. Sharon walked in with no clothes on, only her belly ring and big bouncy titties. Sharon turned to lock the bedroom door and all Ryan noticed was that big ass of hers. Sharon's ass was so big you could sit an ashtray on it while continuing to smoke.

"Come kiss it, baby," he demanded of Sharon to put her lips on him.

"We gonna do it my way, no more giving orders, Mister," She said.

Sharon climbed on the bed, turned her back toward Ryan while he could play with her ass and teased him as she sat on his dick going in and out. She was wet as fuck; she looked back at it while she continued to ride, he watched her grind on him in slow motion. *Damn, that felt so good,* Ryan thought. Sharon slid off turned around and sat on Ryan's face; all that ass covered his face, he could barely breathe. Ryan ate her out while she moaned and groaned, leaning against the headboard. Ryan felt her legs tremble as he sucked her clit 'til she squirted on his face.

"Turn over, babe, and face down," he said.

Sharon's head was buried in the pillow as he slapped her ass a couple times, sticking one finger in her asshole, she squirmed.

"Sharon, relax."

Ryan leaned over, grabbed the KY jelly from the nightstand drawer, lubricated his dick and her asshole.

"What are you about to do back there, Ryan? I don't take it in my ass, you know that," she said whining before he even started.

"Sharon, just relax, it will only hurt entering, and that's it. Loosen up. Talk dirty to me or something," he said while she was getting on his nerves. "Arch your back...that's it!"

Ryan pushed himself into Sharon's ass as she kept squirming each time. He lubricated her some more as he forced himself almost in it.

"Ouch dammit!" Sharon hollered.

*She's about to get on my last nerve*, he thought. *Ava didn't mind at all.*

"I'm almost in it, relax." Ryan felt her ripping apart as he poured more jelly on his dick letting it run in her ass. He pumped hard. After twenty minutes of sweating, he was finally in there. Ryan fucked Sharon gently as she wept on the bed. He ignored her cries and fucked her while squeezing her ass; he pulled out, and then stuck his tongue in her ass to ease her pain. Ryan went back in only to cum in her ass, letting it drip on the bedspread.

"Sharon, sweetheart," he called out.

She looked at him in tears, "I told you to stop, why didn't you? It hurt like hell," she cried.

"Baby, I'm sorry," Ryan said as he tried to comfort her as she got up limping to the bathroom only to run her some bath water. He showered real quickly. "Babe, I'm going to get the kids and take them home early," he said.

"So, you're just going to rip my ass apart and leave?" Sharon pouted.

"I'll be back, I need to go get them settled first."

He tried to touch Sharon and wipe her back, but she refused his help. Not understanding what got her so ill, he said "Fuck it," and left.

*Love and War*

## *The Return of the Beast*

$A$va finished up her last book signing for the weekend in Vegas.

She was surprised from the turnout and all the fans that read her books that came out and showed her some love. The girls came along for a fun-filled weekend and she couldn't be any happier. Alisse also joined in on the festivities.

"Can you believe Ryan dropped the kids off at his mom's for the weekend?" Ava said to Alisse.

"For what? I mean isn't he suppose to be watching them?" Alisse said.

"Ummmm, yes. He is probably with that slut Sharon," Ava put her head down trying not to think about it, only to think about it.

"Alisse, honestly I'm tired I don't know what to do anymore."

Alisse hugged Ava, "Ava, I worry about you. Ryan thinks the grass is greener on the other side let him go there and water it, divorce his ass, and get with Malcolm," Alisse said smiling. "Besides I like him."

The line was getting shorter and shorter and she was glad because her hand had started to hurt. Elaine, Ava's agent, walked over, "I just shut it down!"

"Here, I thought the line was just short," she said.

Angela, Lisa, and Karen came in with Starbucks coffee, just in time to pack things up and head back to the hotel. Ava tried to help Alisse lower the table only to bend over in pain.

"Ava, are you okay?" Alisse and Lisa asked.

"Yeah, I'm good, just pulled a muscle," Ava said. She didn't know what was going on with her body and she was afraid to find out.

Ava and the girls dined at Spago before heading back to Bellagio where they were staying just to relax, freshen up, and then hit the strip. Ava ate a couple bites of her food and wanted to just lie down. She tried to keep an upbeat mood since everyone was there for her.

"Geez, that was great, I think I can go for another round of lamb chops," Karen said with her four month belly poking out.

Ava smiled at the thought of Karen being a mom.

"What you smiling for?" Lisa asked.

"Damn, Lisa, you notice everything," Angela said.

Lisa waved her hand, "Whatever."

*Love and War*

"I was admiring Karen's little belly and can't believe she's going to be a mom," Ava said as they all kind of laughed.

Karen stood up, "I'm fat, ain't I? Tell the truth ladies," then sat back down.

They all waved their hands, "Girl, you still look the same," Alisse stated.

They took their to-go boxes of what was left of the food and headed to the room. Soon as they got in, Ava headed straight for the bed.

"Are we going to the Jubilee show tonight?" Alisse asked.

All the talking they were doing was fading out in Ava's ears. She had to have dozed off for at least thirty minutes.

"Ava, you okay, sis? You don't look so hot," Alisse said putting her hand on Ava's forehead. "Ava, sit up and take these aspirin," she said pulling out two Aleve.

"Alisse, I don't know what's going on, I've been having pain for awhile, I feel dizzy." Ava tried to sit up, only to flop back down. "Give me a minute and let me rest and don't say anything to the girls," she said.

"Ava, promise me when we get back home you will go see a doctor. I'm going with you," Alisse protested. She walked off and Ava heard her tell Angela she had a stomach bug. They agreed to let her rest awhile.

Ava noticed the kids calling her and her mom. She let them all go to voicemail nothing from Ryan like she expected.

Ava remembered Ryan walking over to her as she tried to rest and kissed her on the forehead, his love for her was one of a kind. He woke her up talking about having more kids; the thought of being a mother again was wonderful. They planned the baby shower, picked baby names, and even planned the christening. Ava's life was wonderful; they had beautiful kids, a man she would die for, and a great career at that. Ryan and Ava renewed their wedding vows till death do them part; they shook hands that through anything they'd remain together. Confident in her own skin Ava didn't care what anyone thought about their relationship, no one would and could ever come between them, until that damn Sharon walked into the picture. She couldn't stand her. Ava saw Sharon come towards her with what looked like divorce papers and before she knew it, she tried to kill that bitch, "You whore!" Ava yelled. Ava then choked her "Sharonnnnn," she screamed. "Leave my family alone!" she continued to choke her. "Sharonnnn," Ava yelped while trying to wake up.

"Ava, Ava, Ava," Angela shook her, "Wake up."

"Ava, baby, wake up!" Alisse called out.

Ava opened her eyes looking around the room with her head spinning finally noticing Angela and Alisse, as Karen and Lisa ran into the room.

"What's going on?" Lisa asked.

"Ava was having a dream," Alisse said.

"More like a nightmare, Sharon seems like a problem we need to address when we get back home," Angela said.

"I'm up, sorry guys didn't mean to scare ya'll," Ava said looking at her hands.

Everyone cleared the room so they all could get dressed and head out. Alisse looked back in on Ava again to make sure she was okay.

An hour later they all headed to the limo, first stop was the Jubilee show, then club hopping from Lax, to Club Pure, and then they were going to end the night at Club Chateau. The night life in Vegas was amazing, everyone enjoyed themselves.

"What happens in Vegas stays in Vegas," Lisa yelled out the limo.

The showgirls from the Jubilee show rocked! They even went back stage and learned a few moves. The Club scene at Lax was popping; Chris Brown and his entourage were spotted, along with Rhianna, Britney Spears, and Justin Timberlake. Angela hopped in a cage and danced like a stripper, while Alisse joined her. Ava managed to have fun despite how she was feeling.

They all partied until the sun came up. They had a couple of hours to get to the room and sleep before it was time to head back home.

It was so nice to get back home doing what she did best…write. Ava wrote daily about her everyday life since the surgery; Ava contemplated writing a memoir about her life, calling it "Life is not a Fairytale." The only problem was Ava wasn't sure on how much she wanted to reveal.

Ryan got up before she did and left in a hurry. Abbie and Jaxon, on the other hand, were glad she was home. Abbie stated the weekend was a disaster, Ryan picked them up from his mom only to leave them at home. And to think he fussed Ava out for the same thing, but she guessed the rules didn't apply to him.

Ava climbed on the bed, then wrote some more. She stopped mid-sentence to call Dr. Patel; as soon as she picked her phone up, Alisse was calling.

"Hey, sis."

"Hey, lady, you call your doctor yet?" Alisse asked.

"As a matter of fact, I was about to call him when you called in."

Alisse didn't believe Ava, "Hmmm, I just hope you're not pregnant," she said.

"I hope not, either. Besides you have to have sex in order to get pregnant, Alisse!" Ava said laughing at her comment. "I'll call you back soon."

*Love and War*

Ava dialed Dr. Patel's office and spoke with the front desk about an appointment. They were able to squeeze her in that afternoon. Ava called Alisse back and told her to meet her at the doctor's office at 3:45 p.m., and then texted Ryan to pick up the kids since Abbie had basketball practice.

Thinking about Malcolm, Ava decided to call him. He didn't pick up so she left him a sweet message. Moments later Ava received a text from Malcolm.

MSG: *Hey sweetheart in a long business meeting, it will be awhile before I get out of here, will call you when it's over...missing you*☺

MSG: *Miss you more* ☺...Ava replied.

Ava wished it was so easy to just leave Ryan and be with Malcolm; life throws some wild cards at times. Ava leaned her head back on the headboard thinking...

Finally sitting in the waiting room at Dr. Patel's office, patiently waiting, Alisse walked in and Ava flagged her. They embraced then sat down.

"You just got here?" Alisse asked.

"About five minutes ago."

They sat making small talk waiting on the nurse to call Ava back. Ava was nervous, not knowing what to expect. The last visit wasn't a pleasant experience, so this time she was on edge.

"Ava Decree," the tiny nurse called. Ava followed the nurse as Alisse followed right behind them.

Ava looked at the scale when it read 137, "Oh my, I've gained some weight," she said while covering her mouth.

They went right into the ultrasound room; Dr. Patel took no time and came in with a specialist who was going to perform a series of tests. After a couple minutes of pushing on her abdomen, it was obvious Dr. Patel felt something. Ava knew that look.

The ultrasound was performed, Ava watched Alisse who looked on carefully, and Ava watched the doctor and specialist as they both pointed to the monitor, then looked at each other. Dr. Patel put his hand on his chin. "Go back and look at the area. Scroll to your right," Dr. Patel said.

"Dr. Patel what's going on?" Ava asked nervously. Ava felt herself about to shake off the bed.

"Ava, I'm afraid to say this, but the cancer has reoccurred and it's worse than before," He said.

"What do you mean worse, Doctor?"

"Ava, it has spread beyond your abdomen, which is connected to your lungs and liver. It doesn't look good. I'm sorry."

"So, Dr. Patel what does that mean?" Alisse asked, while trying to read the monitor.

Grabbing Ava's hand, "It means that the cancer is no longer early and will be difficult to treat because it has spread. That's why you were having the symptoms you were," Dr. Patel explained.

Ava didn't know what to think as she lied back on the table. The specialist explained the ovarian cancer while going over

*Love and War*

the ultrasound, pictures, and her diagnosis before the first surgery. He also explained that not all cancer goes away. It can reoccur like hers had. Dr. Patel also asked to speak with her alone; Ava told him whatever he has to say he could say it in front of Alisse.

"Ava, really, by looking at this, the only option is surgery and chemotherapy," he looked at Alisse then Ava again. "I'm sorry, but it's difficult to remove the cancer with surgery since it has spread beyond the abdominal area and there is no guarantee that chemotherapy will eradiate the remaining cancer," Dr. Patel stated trying to remain calm.

Alisse had tears in her eyes, she squeezed Ava's hands as tightly as she could and rubbed her head.

"Dr. Patel, how long do I have?" Ava asked calmly as tears began rolling down her face uncontrollably.

"Ava, I give you less than four months. I'm sorry. I'm so, so sorry," he said hugging her in tears.

"Life just isn't fair! No, my sister is going to be here, we're going to beat this because God has the last say," Alisse yelled out. "No cancer is going to take my sister away from me!" she cried.

"I understand, Alisse, I'm sorry. And, yes, God does has the last say," Dr. Patel reiterated.

The specialist was still in the room, and he touched Ava's hand then left feeling sorry for her. Ava couldn't believe what was happening with her. She was 39-years old. She needed to be there for her kids' sake, the more and more she thought about it, the more she cried and relied on God.

Ava held Alisse tight, all she could think about was her kids, her health, and how long she would be able to fight.

## *When It Rains, It Pours*

Ryan walked in the door as Ava was serving dinner to the kids.

He said his hello to everyone, kissed Ava on the cheek, and asked to talk to her later. Ava turned to Ryan and smiled like something was bothering her.

Ryan sat down with the kids and asked them about school as he joked around with Jaxon. Ryan looked at Ava who was hovering over the sink thinking to himself how in the hell he was going to do this and break the news to her, but it's been a long time coming.

"Do you want something to eat, Ryan?" Ava asked.

"Sure," he said.

Ava fixed Ryan a plate then took it to him at the table. Ryan really didn't have an appetite, but figured he better eat something because he did not know how the night might go.

The kids finished their dinner, then went upstairs to get ready for school the next day and bed. There was silence in the kitchen as Ava went to start some laundry. Ryan ate alone with his thoughts.

After he ate, Ryan headed upstairs to shower. He went in and said good night to the kids, then headed downstairs to talk with Ava who was eating at the table and reading a Vogue magazine.

"Ava, sweetheart, I've got something I want to tell you," Ryan sat down and began to speak.

Ava looked at Ryan waiting for him to talk as he blurted, "I want a divorce."

Ava didn't seem shocked; instead she asked quietly as she continued eating, "Why, Ryan?"

Ryan avoided her question, but went on to say how unhappy he was. The love was gone. "Ava, I haven't touched you in months. You're a good person; I just don't love you anymore. Not like I love Sharon. I'm sorry, but our marriage is over," he managed to say with a deep sense of guilt. Ava got up and threw her plate away, came back and got in his face.

"You bastard, how could you do this to me? Not once have I ever cheated on you. Instead I was there for your every need. The good wife…you're not a man! I hope Sharon makes you happy because what goes around comes around!" Ava said calmly.

That night, they didn't talk to each other. Ryan went and got the divorce agreement he had drafted up as Ava wept at the kitchen table. He handed her the agreement, which stated she could own the house, her car, 50% of their shared account, and 50% of

*Love and War*

stake in royalties' sales of all published books while they were married. She glanced at the documents, looked at him, and then tore the papers up in Ryan's face. The woman that he once loved, the mother of his kids and his wife of thirteen years, had suddenly become a stranger to him.

"I'm sorry, Ava, I never meant to hurt you or waste your time," he said trying to make light of the situation.

Ryan really felt bad for Ava, but couldn't take back how he felt about Sharon. Regardless the kids would be taken care of. Ava cried uncontrollably in front of him and he was kind of relived that she released her emotions. Now that he had finally addressed the divorce with Ava, the future seemed much clearer.

Ryan kindly went upstairs to call Sharon who was thrilled that they didn't have to hide their relationship anymore. Although she was happy that he finally told Ava, she also felt sorry for her.

"Ryan, we can finally be together, aren't you happy?" Sharon asked.

"Yes, sweetheart, I am!" he responded. They said their goodbyes and hung up.

Ryan sat in the recliner as he heard pieces of paper being balled up, he went downstairs to check on Ava who was at the table writing, he went back upstairs and left her alone. Hours later, after he drifted off, Ryan heard the same noise and again. Ava was still at the table writing and balling up paper. Not sure what she was doing, but he went back to sleep quickly because he was tired and had a very eventful evening with Sharon.

Morning came quickly, Ryan felt like he had just laid down. He tried to get up early and leave the house before anyone awoke not wanting to face Ava, but he hit the snooze button one too many times.

Ryan heard the kids down stairs loud as usual, so he got up. He heard Jaxon come up stairs with his big feet.

"Dad, you're coming to Abbie's game later?"

"Yes, I'll be there, where is your sister anyway?"

"Right here, Dad," Abbie said coming up the steps.

Ryan hugged her and said, "Good luck, baby girl."

She smiled and hugged him back; he gave Jaxon a high five and gave both money for later. That was Jaxon's reason for coming to see him.

"You kids have a great day," he said.

Both of them ran downstairs as they heard Ava call for them because Angela was outside. Not sure why Angela picked up the kids, but he guessed she was dropping them off along with Chrissy. Ryan showered to wake up then finished getting dressed to leave for work.

Ryan went downstairs where Ava was waiting for him. Not wanting to argue, he said good morning and poured some coffee. Ava presented him with her divorce agreement and conditions she wanted met. Ryan read the agreement, which sounded feasible:

*Love and War*

1. She at least wanted a 30-day notice before the divorce was final.

2. She also requested that they live as normal of a life as possible for the kids' sake, not wanting them to know what's going on until the 30-day notice.

3. Also Ryan could have the house, cars, furniture, etc., she wanted nothing.

4. Be the best father and husband to their family until they divorce.

5. Ava wanted Ryan to carry her from the bedroom to the front door every morning for 30 days, just to recall how he carried her out when they first wed, that's all she wanted.

Agreeing to all her terms Ryan was puzzled about Ava's last request where she wanted him to carry her for 30 days. Ava asked Ryan to just do it, that's all she asked, just to make the last days together bearable. Ryan looked at Ava's frail face and accepted her odd request. Not anywhere in Ava's agreement did she mention half of her book royalties, Ryan smiled. Not sure how he was going to explain this to Sharon, he still kissed Ava on the cheek and left for work not looking back.

••••••••• ━━━ ••• ━━━ •••••••••

Ava knew her time here on earth was limited, so she planned to prepare herself and her loved ones around her. Ava took a moment after Ryan left, touched her cheek where he kissed her, and cried.

She was already dressed and ready for Alisse to take her to her chemotherapy treatment. Ava didn't know how long she could bear the treatments; they made her sick and she felt worse some days.

There was a knock on the door. She went to let Alisse in and when she opened the door she was startled, "Mom?"

"Ava, baby, I'm so sorry," Elaine said collapsing in her arms.

Ava and her mom cried together, she stood there and looked Ava in the face as Alisse walked in.

"Mom, don't worry about me, I've lived a good life. Just help Alisse take care of my kids," she told her.

Ava closed the door and both of them sat at the table. It was silent at first.

"Ava, what about Ryan? Abbie and Jaxon? Have you told them?" Alisse asked.

"No, and I don't plan to. I don't want them to worry. You two are the only ones that know, right, Alisse?" Ava asked making sure their mom was the only one that knew.

"Yes, I couldn't help it, I felt like mom needed to know. I'm sorry, sis," Alisse said.

Elaine touched Ava's hand, "Baby girl, what am I'm going to do? The thought of losing you is painful," she said.

*Love and War*

"Please, you guys, not a word to anyone, let me make that call. Mom, stop worrying, please," Ava said tearfully.

They all got up to go to her treatment. Ava dazed out the window on the ride there. Alisse kept watching her through the mirror. Ava was thinking that she had a lot to do. She was meeting with Elaine, her agent, later to change her beneficiary, life insurance documents, meet with her pastor, and plan her funeral.

Ava couldn't bear the thought of leaving her kids, they were her world. Ava planned to record herself for memory's sake; to share with them all they needed to know about life.

They arrived at the center, Ava's mom stayed in the car; she couldn't bear to see Ava that way. Ava went to her normal station and what felt like hell only took ten minutes. Alisse helped Ava to the car and when she settled in the seat, Ava laid her head against the window.

Ava texted Malcolm, she really needed to speak with him and let him know what was going on with her. She agreed to meet him later at his place.

---

*F*inally home, all Ava could do was rest. She dismissed Alisse and Elaine, and then called Elaine, her agent, to come over instead of meeting her in a couple of hours.

Hours passed and Elaine found herself in Ava's bedroom crying her eyes out. She told her about her cancer reoccurring and the amount of time she had left. She also decided to put out her memoir and put the final touches on it in the days to come.

Elaine agreed to meet with Ava and her attorney to go over documents regarding her estate, royalties, other sales, and how she would like for ten percent of the proceeds to go to ovarian cancer research.

"What am I going to do without my friend and bestselling author?" Elaine stated looking at Ava. "I just can't believe this. You are just getting started…the movie, memoir, and Abbie fashions," she said rubbing Ava's leg.

"Girl, you'll do just fine, my legacy will still live on through you and Abbie, so pucker up, no goodbyes," Ava said.

After she was sworn to secrecy, Elaine left to handle some things for Ava. Ava felt weak, but needed to keep pressing on.

Ava looked at the time and needed to head to Abbie's game. She'd stop by Malcolm's place later. Ava wanted to keep life for her kids as normal as possible without them worrying about her.

Ava glanced at herself in the mirror and she almost couldn't recognize herself, she looked pale and very afraid of what may happen.

*Love and War*

## Watch How You Treat People

*R*yan was sitting at his desk feeling some type of way thinking about how the kids laughed as he carried Ava from the bedroom to the front door. It was very awkward, they both were clumsy and he almost dropped her. When he carried Ava she just closed her eyes and he couldn't wait to get it over with.

Ryan was thinking 29 more days to go. He called that morning and had Ava dropped from his life insurance policy, which insured a million dollars if something were to happen. Since they were divorcing, he needed to cancel all policies that included her.

"Hey, what's happening, man?" Carl said peeping his head in.

"Come on in. I'm good, bro," Ryan responded.

"Just speaking…on my way to a meeting. How is Ava, Angela claims she hasn't heard from her in days," Carl asked.

"Ava is good, but just to let you know. I did ask Ava for a divorce, so that may be a reason she's been distant," he said.

Before Carl could get a word out, Ryan held up his hands, "Please don't judge."

"Man, come on, what are you doing? Nevermind…it's not my business, although I think you're making a big mistake."

"Well, let me worry about that Carl. I know the girls will have a lot to say because they always do, but this is my life."

Carl left after being paged on the intercom. Not sure why he cared so much, but it was what it was…Ava would find someone else.

Ryan noticed Ricky walking towards his door and wondered what the hell he wanted. Ricky knocked, and then peeped in, "Ryan, I need you to sign off on this expense report for some items I just purchased for the maintenance department," he said.

"Let me take a look at it."

Ricky sat while Ryan glanced at the report, then Ricky lay back in the chair, Ryan guessed he was taking too long because it got dead silent.

"Hey, man, how long you and Sharon being kicking it?" Ricky asked.

"Excuse me?" Ryan said looking over his reading glasses.

"How long have y'all been sleeping together? Since you didn't understand the first question," he repeated in another way.

*Love and War*

    Ryan looked at him and thought, *This boy ain't my friend, so why the small talk?* Ricky was one of those smooth talkers that could talk people out of anything. He was stocky, built, lean, and handsome for a dude. His cockiness is what Ryan didn't like about him. He thought he was God's gift to women.

    Ryan turned his attention back to him, "Sharon and I are just friends, I'm married Ricky."

    "You're getting a divorce right? Ava is a nice looking lady, I hope you're not leaving her for Sharon….yeah, we kick it from time to time," Ricky said with a smirk.

    Ryan hurried and signed Ricky's expense report, then handed it to him just to get him out of his office. Ricky got up about to leave not saying a word.

    "By the way, Sharon won't be stopping by to talk from time to time. Her life just became a little busier," Ryan said.

    Ricky looked back with a grin, "Bad mistake, man, bad mistake," and walked out.

    Not knowing what he meant by his comment, Ryan trusted Sharon, so there was no need to worry. Stomach growling, Ryan couldn't wait to see what Sharon cooked up for lunch. She had the day off and asked him to come over.

An hour later Ryan was sitting at Sharon's kitchen table grubbing down some cream corn, fried pork chops, mashed potatoes, and homemade biscuits. Ryan had to admit the woman knew how to cook. Ava could cook as well, thanks to Ryan's mom, but it was always the same things…casseroles, baked fish, steamed vegetables, and pasta. Ava never knew how to cook collards, which were his favorite, or any other soul food, but she tried.

"You want some more, baby?" Sharon asked.

"No, I'm good; don't want to get too full, besides I want dessert!" Ryan said laughing.

"I'm sure you do, which explains why I'm cooking in heels and just this apron" Sharon said seductively. "Anyway, how is home?"

"Awkward, you know one of Ava's terms is for me to carry her from the bedroom to the front door for 30 days to smooth the process."

"What!" Sharon gasped.

"Yes, I agreed to it, not knowing why. Today was the first day and it was crazy and weird, I almost dropped her," he said.

Sharon laughed and thought carrying Ava downstairs until the divorce was absurd.

"It would be funny if you dropped her, Ryan," Sharon said with a grin. "Well, no matter what tricks she plays for the next couple of weeks, Ava still has to face the divorce," Sharon said scornfully.

Walking towards Ryan and sitting on his lap naked, wearing nothing but the apron.

Sharon said, "I can't wait to get you to myself," as she kissed his neck then started unbuttoning his shirt. Ryan heard his phone go off, but ignored it. Sharon stood up and threw the apron on the floor, revealing her navel ring and nicely shaved Brazilian wax.

Ryan immediately kissed her enlarged clitoris as it looked so good to him, but before he could go any further his phone went off a couple more times. He grabbed it just in case there was an emergency and noticed it was from work. Ryan listened to the voice message and it was Andrew demanding Ryan get back to work, there was an emergency meeting with the head chief and he needed to be there in twenty minutes.

"Shit!" Ryan said.

"What is it?" Sharon asked.

"Work, I have to get to an emergency meeting."

Sharon looked disappointed. Ryan kissed her a couple more times.

"Rain check, I'll have to make it up to you...sorry, but I have to leave," he said grabbing his keys while he was rock hard heading for the door.

Sharon walked behind Ryan looking sad, "You better!" she said.

Ryan jumped in his ride and hit the brakes. He checked himself in the mirror then called Andrew back.

"Hey man, what's going on?" he asked.

"Something about finances and the expense report that was signed off for Ricky this morning. You know anything about that?" Andrew asked.

"Yes! Damn it, I signed it...I hope his ass isn't trying to set me up. I'm on my way!" Ryan said hanging up.

*I just hope that fool didn't do anything stupid for his sake,* he said to himself.

---

Ava was down for the count after her chemo treatment; she didn't know how long she could continue the treatments because they made her worse every time. Dr. Patel thought the cancer was getting worse.

Ava felt so sick that she couldn't move. She managed to get up after hearing the door bell. Ava peeked out the window and it was Angela.

"What was she doing here?" she mumbled.

Ava went down stairs and opened the door.

*Love and War*

"Well, hello stranger, is everything okay?" Angela asked looking around walking into the house.

Ava closed the door, "Yes, why you ask?"

Angela looked at her, "Because, Ava, you look like hell and I haven't heard from you in weeks. I usually hear from you every day. Besides you're not answering your phone. I waited this long to stop by, thinking you needed time for God knows what," Angela said loudly while pacing the floor. "So, girl, what's up?"

Ava immediately burst out into tears, grabbed Angela by the arm and moved her to the couch.

"Ava, what is it? Did I do something or say something wrong?" Angela asked.

"No, no," she said between sniffs. Ava confided in Angela about her doctor visit after her trip from Vegas, the cancer, and her dying. She needed to talk to someone and it was her.

Angela hugged Ava, rocked her and cried. Angela took it pretty hard. Ava asked her to keep it to herself, no telling Carl, no one. She didn't understand, but Ava told her she simply didn't want anyone to worry, especially her kids.

"Oh my, I'm so sorry, Ava."

"Angela on top of that Ryan asked me for a divorce," Ava said.

Angela jumped out of her seat, "He did what? That bastard...how could he, Ava!"

Ava explained to Angela all that she's been dealing with. No support beside Alisse, her mom, now her.

"You three are the only ones that know, Angela, aside from Elaine, my agent and Malcolm. I told him last night, so please promise me you won't get emotional and say anything. Not to Karen or Lisa, they will go overboard. You're the only one out of the girls I'm confiding in."

"How did Malcolm take it?"

"Not so good. He prayed with me, made me feel good, and said he never met anyone like me ever."

Ava stood by the window and watched her neighbor in the yard. It would be the little things that she cherished the most that she would miss.

"You know, Angela, I've lived a good 39-years, and I just wish I had more time. My hair is beginning to fall out, my marriage is fading, so what else is next?" Ava blurted.

Angela put her hand on Ava's shoulder, "Ava, I'll be here to help you through this journey. Abbie and Jaxon will be just fine and I'll make sure of that. Ryan won't have that bitch looking after them, that's for sure," Angela said.

"Thank you, Angela!"

Ava also updated Angela on her plan to leave everything to her kids. Alisse will be the guardian of their estate and their trustee, and she added Angela to co-parent as well since she was their Godmother. Ava had her will and her accounts changed and

*Love and War*

added a new beneficiary. She also told her Ryan wouldn't be getting a dime and for him to think that he's entitled to her book money was absurd.

Ava yelled, "I wrote those damn books, not him!"

Ava told Angela about Ryan taking her off of his insurance policy and changing his beneficiary. The company called Ava after Ryan made those changes to make sure she was aware that she was no longer added.

"Damn, he's something else. That's cold, Ava. But you're smarter and Ryan won't know what hit him!" Angela said in disbelief. "He doesn't know about the cancer, but takes you off of his insurance policy, change his beneficiary as well? But he asked about your royalties in the divorce terms? He got some nerves. That's just like a greedy ass black man, though!"

They sat there for a while reminiscing about the past and how they were going to miss each other. Angela offered to go with Ava to pick out wigs, her treatments, and anything else she could do. Ava knew she could always count on Angela.

"Angela, please help look after my kids along with Ryan and Alisse. I've been recording daily to leave them with something, but Abbie is growing up into a beautiful young lady and Jaxon a handsome young man."

"Ava, don't worry, you'll be proud of them. Alisse and I will make sure they will be well off. I got you!" Angela said.

"I know girl, I know. I just need to be reassured."

Angela ended up cooking as they ate and sipped tea. Hours passed by and Ava didn't care. Before she knew it the kids were home and she tried to be upbeat and entertain them, so they wouldn't think anything was off.

Ava was trying to enjoy every moment she had left to spend with Abbie and Jaxon. Ava told them she loved them every day and made sure she kissed and hugged them every chance she got.

*Love and War*

## *It's All or Nothing*

Ava got up and prepared breakfast. She was moving slower than usual. Ava stood by the stove in pain, but didn't say anything as the kids were coming down.

"Mom, what's wrong? You look awful," Abbie said with a concerned look on her face.

"Baby, I'm fine. You kids hurry and eat," she said.

"Mom, I'm worried about you. You're losing weight, you on a diet again?" Jaxon asked.

"Kids, I'm fine and yes, Jaxon, I'm dieting," she said. "Do I look that bad?" Ava asked standing in front of them with her hand on her hip.

"No, Mom, you look great, just smaller," Abbie said intervening.

Ava saw Ryan come down the steps with his briefcase from the corner of her eye and Jaxon jumped from the table, took her hand, and then ran to the bedroom.

Ryan followed them as both kids watched Ryan carry Ava down the steps. Ava wrapped her arms around Ryan's neck, then leaned on Ryan's chest.

Abbie was clapping, "It's nice to see Mom and Dad this way," she said.

"Yeah, that's how you carry a woman, Dad," Jaxon said chiming in on the action.

Ava could smell Ryan's favorite cologne that she bought a dozen times, "Black" by Ralph Lauren. She closed her eyes, then whispered to him, "Please don't tell our kids about the divorce." Ryan nodded, feeling somewhat upset by what Ava said, but continued walking through the sitting room to the door, where he gently put her down.

Jaxon gave Ryan a high five, "Jaxon, I suggest you carry me tomorrow," Abbie joked.

"Girl, please," Jaxon joked back with Abbie.

Ava managed to clean the kitchen while everyone was preparing to leave for the morning. After she took her medication, she climbed back in bed. Ava felt weak and opted out of going to her chemo treatment.

Hours later she awakened to her phone going off; it was Lisa wondering where she'd been hiding. Lisa and Karen have been worrying about Ava. Ava confided in Lisa about the divorce and she went off the handle, another reason why Ava couldn't tell

*Love and War*

her or Karen about the cancer. Karen may be white, but she was one to be reckoned with.

"Ava, fuck Ryan! Hell, you got a man! I suggest you get it popping with ole boy. What's his name again?" Lisa asked.

"Malcolm, Lisa."

"That's right, from the picture, Malcolm reminds me of Robin Thicke," Lisa said laughing. "Blurred Lines" she started singing.

"Lisa, you're crazy, anyway I have to go I'm going to meet up with Mr. Thicke as we speak," Ava said mocking Lisa.

"Alright, chick, we'll get together later for dinner," she said.

Ava finally got up and managed to get dressed. She adjusted her wig, the one Angela selected last week, which kind of looked like her real hair. The wig was hot and Ava hated it. She looked at herself in the mirror and wanted to break down; Ava quickly turned her head to keep from looking at herself.

Ava had to hurry she promised Malcolm she would meet him for lunch since he had the day off.

Ava drove the long way to Malcolm's condo not feeling her best, so she took her time, but figured she'd make the best of her time here. Ava spoke with her mom and Alisse on the drive there to kill time. Alisse was the best sister in the world; she was handling a lot of things for Ava.

Ava got to Malcolm's place and he greeted her with a dozen roses, mixed with lilies, a periwinkle, a mimosa, a lemon blossom, and a honeysuckle.

She immediately fell in his arms and teared up. This man was heaven sent when she needed him the most.

"Malcolm, thank you! They are just gorgeous, I'm so flattered, but why the different flowers?" she asked. Malcolm pulled out a piece of paper then asked Ava to sit and began explaining.

"Ava what I'm about to read is something from the heart. A reason for the different flowers for a special lady," Malcolm said. He sat next to Ava, turned towards her and looked her dead in her eyes.

*"Ava, sweetheart, I'm not sure how we ended up here at this moment in time. Maybe it was destined for us to meet each other that day in the restaurant, but ever since then we've become closer each day. Not sure what the future holds or if there is a future for us, but I do know that I care for you deeply and hope and pray we have more time with each other.*

*2 Roses (red) - Passion/Love*

*2 Roses (coral) - Desire*

*2 Roses (pink) - Grace and Sweetness*

*2 Roses (dark pink) - Thankfulness*

*2 Roses (white) - Purity*

*2 Roses (pale pink) - Joy*

*Love and War*

> *Lillie's - Purity of the heart, honor*
> *Periwinkle - Sweet remembrance*
> *Mimosa - Secret love*
> *Lemon Blossom - Fidelity in love, I promise to be true until the day you die*
> *Honeysuckle - Bond of love, Ava. I love you!*
> *Ava there are so many flowers that symbolize my love and affection for you that this is nothing. This arrangement says it all. Ava, sweetheart, I love you."*

After Malcolm's heartfelt words, Ava hugged him. She was so emotional. She then took his hand, "Malcolm, I love you, too," she told him as they embraced and kissed passionately. Ava couldn't remember the last time she felt like that.

"Malcolm, thank you for everything, and I do mean everything. I was just looking for a friend to talk to, but you ended up being so much more." Ava wiped tears from her face and his face as she continued. "I may be here months from now, even years, who knows, but I do know you've shown me love still exists."

They both sat there in silence for the next fifteen minutes while she laid her head on his chest. Malcolm caressed Ava's hair, which made her uneasy because of the wig.

"Take it off," Malcolm said.

"Huh?" Ava said caught off guard.

"Take it off. The wig. I don't care what you or your hair looks like. I love you for you, Ava," Malcolm said calmly.

Ava couldn't believe she was doing this. She slowly took the wig off. Malcolm watched as she began removing the cap. Ava sat there feeling embarrassed, not pretty, and ashamed. Her hair had come out leaving patches of bald spots. The only person that saw her hair was Angela. This was something she should be sharing with her husband, not another man.

"Thank you for taking it off. Ava you're still stunning, beauty at its worst and its best...that you are," he said.

Although Ava didn't feel beautiful, Malcolm made her feel like the First Lady of the
United States of America. She stood and walked over to the mirror Malcolm had in his dining area to put her wig back on.

"Here, let me help you, Ava," Malcolm said walking over to help her.

Once Ava's wig was back on her head, she turned to Malcolm who was admiring her. She couldn't help but to ask "What?"

"Nothing, you're a trooper, you know that! Through the odds of battling cancer, a divorce, taking care of your kids, family, and friends, I really admire you," he said.

"Malcolm, just promise me whatever happens you won't forget me. I just hope you find someone as genuine as you are to

*Love and War*

me. I'm not dead yet and maybe I won't be, but I want nothing but the best for you," Ava said.

He nodded, they both smiled then embraced.

"Shall we?" he asked.

"Yes…let's go eat!" Ava said.

*Bianca Harrison*

## *My Sister's Keeper*

Angela couldn't help but think about what Ava was going through 24/7. It made her sad to know her friend was dying and she couldn't do anything about it or tell anyone, not even Carl, because she promised Ava.

The thought of Ryan's actions made her sick to her stomach.

Angela did accompany Ava to a couple of her chemo sessions until she stopped going. Ava figured if she was going to die, she'd rather do it without chemotherapy because it made her even sicker and really didn't help.

Angela heard the door open and walked into the kitchen meeting Carl and Chrissy.

"Hey fam, how are ya?" she said to the both of them.

"Good," Carl and Chrissy said at the same time.

*Love and War*

She kissed both of them cherishing every moment. Ava's situation had her thinking twice about family and life.

Angela sat on the bar stool making small talk with Carl who looked frustrated. Chrissy ran upstairs to practice her dance routine for a school play.

"Today was hell, Angela. I had two meetings regarding upcoming projects that will require me to work closely with Ricky. He's cool, but shady at the same time, I have to watch him," Carl said.

"What do you mean shady?" Angela asked.

"He's a manipulator, arrogant, and cocky. He got Ryan wrote up, not sure what happened, but Ricky got Ryan to sign off on an expense report that was rigged with stuff that didn't pertain to work. Ryan didn't read it or look at it carefully and just signed his name. Ricky never went to Ryan to sign off on anything, but this time he did."

"Well that's Ryan's ass; he should have read it, I have no sympathy for the guy," Angela looked at Carl and shrug her shoulders.

Angela watched Carl looking in the fridge, after not finding anything to eat; he poured himself a shot of Hennessy.

"What's for dinner?" he asked.

"Pizza, I guess. I'll order one in a few," Angela grabbed the pizza menu off the refrigerator then dialed the number. It took all of five minutes to call in. Carl sat on the stool beside her.

"Did you know Ryan asked Ava for a divorce?" He said.

"Yes, there's a lot going on with Ava and its sad how he's treating her," she said. "Ryan will get what's coming to him sooner or later," she added.

"What's going on with Ava?" Carl asked.

"Something personal. She swore me to secrecy," Angela said as her eyes began to swell up. The thought of her friend's pain brought tears to her eyes.

"Okay....anyway, whatever it is, we need to stay out of their business and let them handle it, okay, Angela?" Carl stated looking over at Angela.

Angela smiled and nodded her head. They heard the door bell ring and thought it was the delivery guy, but Chrissy ran to the door like it was for her, instead it was Lisa.

"What brings you by, chick?" Angela asked her.

"Just stopping by the neighbor," Lisa said smiling.

"Yeah, right," Carl and Angela said as he excused himself.

Angela grabbed Lisa a bottle of water from the fridge. She looked like she was coming from the gym and exhausted.

Lisa sat on the stool, "Girl, did Ava call you?"

Angela shook her head "No, why?"

"Anyhow Ava and Malcolm was having lunch and ran into Ms. Thang, Sharon the whore," Lisa said.

Angela laughed like hell as Lisa kept using her hands as motion signals.

*Love and War*

"Ava said Sharon walked over to the table and spoke, being nosy summing up Malcolm. Ava asked her why she was there and was she planning on going after Malcolm like she did Ryan and home girl got mad!" Lisa added getting mad herself. "Now, Angela, how the hell do you get mad sleeping with that woman's husband!"

Angela immediately grabbed the phone and called Ava putting her on speaker phone, the phone rang a couple times before Ava picked up.

"Hey, chick, Lisa just told me about Sharon, what the hell happened?" Angela asked.

Ava was so agitated and upset explaining how Sharon walked over to the table trying to play nice, but really being nosey trying to figure out who Malcolm was. She politely told Sharon to leave, that she was on a date.

"Angela, she had the nerve to say, *Good then the divorce shouldn't take any time!*" Ava said through the speaker.

Carl ran downstairs after hearing the doorbell and answered to the delivery guy. He walked into the kitchen and heard Ava talking, he tried to speak, but Angela shhhhd him.

Ava continued and promised Sharon was going to get what's coming to her.

"Girl, don't worry about her, people who bring misery to other people are miserable and will always be miserable," Lisa said.

Angela told Ava not to let that bother her and promised to call her back. Carl stood there trying to figure out what was going on.

"Babe, Sharon invited herself to Ava's table while she was having lunch gloating about the divorce, now tell me that ain't foul?" Angela said to Carl.

"Angela, stay out of it; let Ava handle it. I hate what's going on, that girl, Sharon, is a mess; she's in Ryan's face one minute, then in Ricky's face the next. Anyway y'all ladies carry on," Carl said taking his plate of food upstairs.

Lisa and Angela both discussed the situation and Angela almost let it slip that Ava was sick. She caught herself and changed the subject. They talked about Karen and throwing her a baby shower in a couple of months, one thing was for sure, they would all remain close and that was because of Ava, her spirit was warm and genuine.

After Lisa left, Angela sat downstairs alone and ate a couple slices of pizza, until Chrissy ran in interrupting her thoughts.

"Mom, you love me right?" Chrissy asked showing all her pearly whites.

"Child, what do you want?" she asked knowing it was something.

*Love and War*

"Can you buy me an iPad?" she asked as serious as she could be.

Angela looked at her like "seriously?" she cut a smile and said, "NO!"

"Please...I could have yours and you get a new one," she begged.

"Chrissy, I'll think about it," Angela said so she could hush.

Chrissy gave Angela the biggest hug ever then planted kisses all over her like she said yes. The joy of being an only child. Angela couldn't help, but love her back.

*Bianca Harrison*

## *Too Good to Be True*

*I*t was a rainy and wet day, all Ryan wanted to do was sleep in. He woke up to Sharon banging pots and pans in the kitchen. Ryan started to yell at her to quiet down a little, but figured he'll let it be and put his head under the pillow. Ryan was so exhausted from a long week at work and being out late last night.

Ryan occasionally stayed at Sharon's place on the weekends now that his divorce was in proceedings. He moved a few pieces to Sharon's since she cleared space for him in her closet and garage, but there were little things that she did that were starting to get on Ryan's nerves, which gave him second thoughts.

Ryan was also a little upset with Sharon announcing to everyone about them being a couple last night at an engagement party for one of her close friends. Ryan wasn't ready to meet her entire family and friends just yet, he's not divorced; but Sharon insisted people would find out about them soon. Sharon also gave a

*Love and War*

toast to the lovely couple, then toasted to their future, which turned the focus to them.

Just then Sharon was in the hallway heading towards the bedroom. Ryan played possum not wanting to be bothered. The bedroom door opened, and then he heard her steps coming towards the bed.

"Ryan, Ryan," Sharon whispered while shaking him. Ryan's head was still buried under the pillow as he mumbled, "Hmmm…"

"I cooked your favorite breakfast," Sharon said.

Ryan mumbled again as he managed to remove the pillow from his head. He noticed Sharon sitting on the bed still in her gown with a tray full of French toast, cheese eggs, grits, bacon, and grapefruit juice. The tray full of food looked fantastic, but he was still upset with her. Ryan sat up as Sharon placed the tray on his lap as he began to eat.

"How did you sleep?" she asked.

"Fine."

"That's it?" Sharon said noticing Ryan looking at her, "Are you still upset with me about last night?"

"I am! Sharon I can't be all out in the open like you want me to be until the divorce is final with Ava."

Ryan noticed Sharon folding her arms ready to explode, so he had to fix the situation quickly.

"Babe, I know we are taking risks going here and there, but I don't want it to bite me in the ass later."

Sharon stood up, while he continued to eat. "Ryan, you're contradicting yourself. We're out all the time, not in town, but people do see us, besides my friends and family know nothing about you," Sharon said, like that was supposed to make him feel better.

Ryan finished his plate then put the tray on the stand. He was about to get up and shower when Sharon came out of her gown and hopped in bed.

This was one time Ryan was not in the mood for sex, which seemed all he and Sharon had in common these days. She fondled Ryan, while he just sat there not even excited by her touch.

"Ryan, babe, stop acting like a puss!" she said.

Again Ryan didn't budge. Sharon then got under the sheets, pushed Ryan back with her hand, and started slurping on his wood. This usually gets him going, but this time it did nothing. Sharon slurped, slobbered, sucked Ryan's balls, and then finally came up for air when he didn't respond back.

"Baby, what is it?" Sharon whined.

"Nothing" Ryan responded. "Turn around and get on all fours," he demanded. Ryan knew exactly what would get him in the mood. He threw Sharon a pillow because she was going to need it only for her to look back and give him the evil eye.

"You really want this, Sharon."

*Love and War*

"Yes, babe, I do!" she said moaning like an owl in heat.

Ryan played with Sharon and got her wet by entering the tip of his dick in her. She moaned for Ryan not to stop. He inserted a finger in her ass while he gyrated in her. It had to feel good to her because she didn't tell him to stop. While Sharon moaned out loud, Ryan grabbed the lukewarm liquid and rubbed his dick. He poured some on Sharon's ass, sat back, and then jabbed his dick in her ass hole as hard as he could.

"Ouch!" she screamed and squirmed. "Ryan you're hurting me!" Sharon yelled. She yelled some more and screamed for Ryan to stop.

Ryan pumped slower, and then his rhythm sped up. Ryan poured more liquid on her to make it easier.

"Baby, you said you wanted this. You didn't mean it? I don't like it when you lie to me." Ryan said in between strokes as sweat ran down like water on his face dripping everywhere.

"No, Ryan, baby, please stop, you're hurting me!" Sharon hollered.

Ryan heard a knock on the door.

"Mom, are you okay, open up!" Tiffany cried outside the door.

"Baby, mommy is okay, go back to your room," Sharon said calmly.

Tiffany knocked a couple more times, and then it got quiet.

Ryan heard Sharon's cries, just when he was going to explode. He pulled out, slapped her ass, as cum dripped from her ass to the sheets.

"Get out, Ryan! Get the fuck out now!" Sharon screamed as tears flooded the sheets. She then put a pillow in between her legs.

"What the hell is wrong with you, Sharon?" Ryan asked acting stupid.

"Ryan, don't you dare act stupid! You fucked me when I told you to stop. What has gotten into you?" she yelled.

"So, now I'm a rapist, Sharon? Is that it? Damn you! You asked for it, so I gave it to you," Ryan said cold-heartedly heading for the shower.

Ten minutes later Ryan came out only to find Sharon in the recliner in her robe. She got up, shot him a look, and walked past him slamming the bathroom door behind her.

Ryan threw on his clothes, grabbed his keys, and then left as he passed Tiffany sitting outside her door in the hallway.

*Hours later Ryan found himself interacting with his family. He played basketball with the kids who had a blast. Ryan noticed Ava slept most of the time he was there.

*Love and War*

Ryan was still cordial, although Ava knew where he'd been all night. She didn't say anything.

Ryan went into the kitchen and asked Abbie about Ava. "Is Mom okay?" he said.

"Yes, Dad, she's not feeling well and she's tired, that's all," Abbie said.

Ryan returned and sat on the sofa across from Ava as he watched her sleep for some odd reason. He noticed Ava changed her hair color, the wrinkles in her face, how pale she had become, and the color of her nails and realized he hadn't looked at her in a very long time. He had not noticed her changing body.

Ryan sat there thinking how much he had put her through over the last couple of months and how it was affecting her mentally. Ava squirmed on the couch, only to doze back off.

Finally he got up and headed towards the kitchen to cook, something he rarely did. He looked in the fridge then the freezer and nothing. Ryan also looked in the pantry and grabbed a couple cans of salmon, he figured salmon patties it would be. Ryan started some rice, prepared the salmon, then placed them in the frying pan.

Ryan looked down at his vibrating phone and saw a picture Andrew sent him of Ricky and Sharon having dinner.

"That bitch!" Ryan mumbled.

He went into the garage and quickly called Andrew.

"Yo man, what the hell is this?"

"Chill man, I saw your girl and Ricky having dinner on the patio outside of Lucky's, they didn't see me though," Andrew stated.

"She isn't my girl!" he said.

"Whatever man, everyone knows you're both hitting that, you don't want to believe she's involved with Ricky, but there's your proof. Anyway keep this between me and you," Andrew said.

"Whatever!" Ryan said and hung up.

Andrew is full of shit. He'll be in Ricky's face tomorrow then my face the next day. Ryan could see why Ricky had it out for him trying to get him fired and all, but his little game is over!

Ryan heard someone at the door and noticed Ava. "Are you cooking? This salmon is burning!" Ava said.

Ryan ran inside turned the stove off then fanned the smoke alarm.

"Shit!" the kids ran downstairs yelling like the house was on fire.

"Dad, what were you trying to cook?" Jaxon asked.

"Dinner," he said.

Ryan threw out the food including the boiling rice.

"So, what now?" Abbie asked.

"Chinese food!" he said.

He knew it was Ava's second favorite food and asked her if she wanted to join them, Ava said no that she wasn't in the mood for going out. Ryan figured he'd call and have it delivered.

*Love and War*

Ava left the room and he noticed how small she had become, at that moment he started blaming himself. Ryan shook the feeling and then turned his attention back to the picture on his phone Andrew sent. Ryan stared at the picture like he was looking for something, which only showed Sharon and Ricky sitting close together at a table. He was furious!

Ava walked in noticing Ryan, then the doorbell rung.

"I got it!" Jaxon ran to the door like he had money. Ryan grabbed his wallet, then smiled at Ava as he walked pass her.

They all sat and ate at the table like a family, something that Ryan missed. They all engaged in small talk and it gave him a chance to see what was going on with his kids, even Ava talked, although it was a little awkward knowing they'll be divorced soon. Ryan knew it was tough on her, but they both did well in playing their part.

After dinner, Ryan grabbed a cold beer and headed to the sitting room to watch the football game.

Ava peeped in, "Thank you for dinner," she said.

"No problem," he responded.

Ryan watched Ava walk off and followed her with his eyes. He didn't know what went wrong between them, but he wasn't trying to make it right. Ryan's focus turned back to Sharon and that damn picture.

Ryan decided to call Sharon. He dialed her number and it went straight to voicemail. He dialed it again this time it kept ringing. The third time he just left a message.

*"Hey babe I'm just calling to check on you and Tiffany. I'm really sorry if I hurt you and how I left things. Call me when you get this message, I love you,"* he said, then ended the call.

Ryan wondered if he was doing the right thing by divorcing Ava for Sharon. Both women have great qualities, but did he know Sharon well enough to be with her? He wondered.

*Love and War*

## ***Friends until the End***

*A*ngela sat there at the restaurant anxious for the girls to arrive. It was Lisa's birthday and they all decided to do brunch. Angela bought them all gifts to show how much she appreciated them in her life.

Angela looked at her watch wondering why they were all so late, but realized she was early because her battery in her watch had stopped! She sat there for about fifteen more minutes and saw Alisse walking towards the table followed by Ava.

"Hey, ladies," Angela said getting up to greet them both. Angela gave Ava a big hug. Angela noticed Ava didn't have her wig on, but a scarf instead.

"I love the scarf, lady. So how are you, Ava?" Angela asked before the rest of the girls got there.

"I'm good, Angela, but could be better." Ava said loosening up the scarf around her head. "You like? That wig was making my head sweat," she said smiling.

"Yes it's very stylish and so are you. I'm glad you could make it. I told you we could have come to you," Angela said putting one hand on top of Ava's hand.

Ava just smiled. She excused herself to the restroom. Alisse stood up to walk with her.

"I got it, sis," Ava said walking off.

Alisse turned her focus to Angela who was almost in tears.

"Angela, it's getting worse. I don't know if I can watch my sister leave me like this! It's not fair!" Alisse said as tears ran down her face.

"Alisse, life isn't fair," Angela said wiping her tears. "We can't do this, not right here. Gather yourself together. Ava would have a fit if she knew we both were not taking this well, all we can do is be there for her."

They both took out their compact mirrors and patted their face just in time as the other girls walked in.

Angela adjusted the table so Karen could sit at the end in case she needed to go to the restroom. They all greeted one another. Ava came back to the table and cracked a smile.

"Happy Birthday, Lisa!" Ava said hugging her.

"What is this new do Ava? The scarf? I kind of like it!" Lisa said pulling on it, as Ava held on tight not wanting it to come off.

"Trying something new, that's all," Ava replied.

*Love and War*

The waiter brought over a bottle of wine as they all watched Lisa open her gifts. Lisa got sentimental then gave the girls individual speeches on how much she enjoyed their friendship.

The waiter came back over and proceeded with their orders. After the gentleman left, Angela told the girls she also had something for them, too.

She pulled out the bag from her huge purse and handed them each a tiny box that contained a keepsake necklace. The necklace read "friends" on the back of the heart shaped pendant and opens with a group picture of them all from her success gathering a few months ago.

"Aw, Angela, this is really nice. I'm flattered," Alisse said as she looked at the necklace.

"I love you, Angela," Ava said smiling at the photo.

Angela watched each of the girls admire their necklace and was glad to have them as part of her life.

"How thoughtful," Lisa said.

"Yeah, how thoughtful of you, Angela, I love you all to pieces," Karen said bringing her body and belly over to kiss Angela on the cheek.

"I just want you all to know how much I appreciate you all. Never had girlfriends like you all before. Life is not promised and I cherish each moment with you ladies," Angela said.

They all then toast with wine and bread from the bread basket the waiter brought over. They did a bit of catch up and took a trip down memory lane for a minute. It was so much laughter at that table Angela thought those people were going to kick them out.

Finally their food arrived. Angela watched Ava eat a little then play with the rest of her food. She felt helpless, like she needed to be doing more for her. Ava caught Angela looking at her and gave her a slight smile. Angela continued to eat when she noticed this big booty woman sitting across from them only to realize it's that damn Sharon.

At that moment Angela didn't want to turn the attention to her and cause a scene, she just played it off and kept eating. Lord knows she wanted to go jam the bitch.

"Lisa, what do you have planned later?" Angela asked.

"My boo and I are going to the Jazz festival over on Clayton and I can't wait!" Lisa said in excitement.

Ava stood up and excused herself again back to the restroom as Alisse also excused herself as well.

"Angela, what do you keep staring at?" Karen asked.

"That bitch at that table! How dare she show her face in public?"

"Who?" Karen demanded to know.

Angela didn't say a word, but took a sip of her wine. Lisa nudged Angela on the arm. Angela turned around noticing Lisa and Karen waiting on an answer, just then Ava and Alisse were walking back towards the table when Ava bumped into Sharon.

"Oh, shit!" Angela jumped up walking towards them as Lisa followed behind her while Karen managed to get up from the table.

Angela got there as they started bickering with one another.

"My, my, my, what do we have here? Is this your entourage?" Sharon said as Lisa and Angela approached them.

"Is there a problem?" Lisa asked confused.

"No, Lisa, this is the bitch that's been screwing around with Ryan, that's all. Slut bucket!" Ava said.

"Home wrecker Sharon? Oh, hell naw, Ava, we should beat her ass!" Lisa said getting heated.

"Bitch, who you calling a home wrecker?" Sharon scolded at Lisa. "As I recall Ryan pursued me," Sharon said.

At that moment people started turning their attention towards them. Sharon's crew who came in with her also walked over and asked what was going on.

Ava explained to them and everyone else in the restaurant what was going on and what a low class whore Sharon was. One of Sharon's friends stated they had no clue Ryan was married. The other girl who came with her grabbed her purse and left. She said she didn't want to be a part of Sharon's mess.

"Ava, Ryan is no longer your problem. Give him his divorce and move on sweetheart, walking around here with that do rag on your head. You think you're black? You ain't black, chick!" Sharon said with so much attitude and hatred like Ryan was actually married to her.

"Bitch, you got some nerve trying to insult me when you've been sleeping with my husband! I don't have to act or be black to be married to a black man, that's what you call ignorance Sharon! Every dog has its day and yours is coming real soon!" Ava snapped back.

Alisse defended Ava and told Sharon, "What goes around comes around. The same way she got him, will be the same way she loses him!"

Sharon kept talking smack and Ava wanted to tear into her. Angela grabbed Ava just in time because she was going to hurt Sharon.

All of a sudden Lisa got in Sharon's face and called her every word there was from tramp stamp to a whore spreader. Angela tried to diffuse the situation when management stepped in. They all headed back to their table to collect the check.

"Don't worry Ava; I'm going to beat her ass for you, that's a foul woman. One thing I can't stand is a trifling whore!" Lisa said.

"Oh trust me; she's going to get it!" Angela said. "Right now this isn't the place or time."

"You see her friends left her. They had no clue how trifling she was," Alisse said.

*Love and War*

They all watched Sharon twist her ass out the restaurant, and then she gave them all the middle finger as she exited.

Angela couldn't believe what just happened! Ava put her head on the table as Karen rubbed her back.

"Why Ava got to act black cause she snagged Ryan, I mean she's crazy," Alisse said.

"Lisa, I just got one word for you, whore spreader?" Angela said laughing.

"Girl, that's a bitch who spreads their legs open to anything," Lisa said. None of the girls had a clue what that meant.

Poor Karen she was getting upset because she couldn't do anything pregnant. Angela just knows she would have swung on Sharon in that restaurant. She was one white girl a sister didn't want to mess with.

Lisa wanted to fight; all she talked about was going to Sharon's house. Angela just knew in the end Ava would get the last laugh and Sharon would be the laughing stock.

When you do wrong it always comes back to bite you in the ass. Sharon was one of those women who cares only about herself. God would see to it that she end up by herself, after it's all said and done.

*Bianca Harrison*

## *Preparing for Takeoff*

Ava watched the kids leave for school and wondered how they would adjust to life without her. She prayed every day that her kids would be just fine. The feeling Ava had knowing her time was limited was painful.

Ryan came downstairs looking for his briefcase as Ava pointed to the chair it was in. Ryan grabbed the briefcase just as everything fell out.

"Shit!" he said.

Ava walked over and helped him gather the documents. She had her hand on a folder as Ryan's hand touched hers. As awkward as it was, Ava quickly moved her hand.

"Ava, I'm so sorry for making you uncomfortable," Ryan said.

Ava burst out into tears as her hands covered her face, then she leaned up against the chair. Ryan rushed to her side only to console her and tell Ava how sorry he was about everything. With

*Love and War*

all that she's been going through, everything seemed to make her cry.

As Ryan hugged Ava, she wiped her tears only to get close enough to smell Ryan's scent. As Ryan consoled and held her, it brought back so many memories and reminded her of the Ryan she fell in love with. After that quick flash back, Ava pushed him away. Ryan stood there with his hands up as she walked off. Ava looked back and noticed Ryan still standing there, but kept walking. Moments later Ava heard the garage door and Ryan pull out the drive way. Ava was so emotional and stressed out about everything.

Ava pulled herself together, headed upstairs and pulled out the camcorder. She went into Abbie's room first, pulled out her photo album, set the recorder, and sat in a chair. Ava decided to record herself for Abbie and Jaxon's sake hoping this will help them understand why she didn't tell them she was sick and what the cancer had done to her.

The recorder was on; Ava proceeded as she took off her wig then started to talk.

*Baby girl, this is your mom speaking. Oh, how I love you and Jaxon so much, you guys are my pride and joy. Your mom is sick, sweetheart. I have ovarian cancer and was given a short time because of how badly it's attacked my body. You see my head, I've lost all my hair, my weight has dropped, which is why I've been sleeping so much. But through it all I didn't want you guys to ever worry about me, I will be just fine.*

Ava paused in between talking, cried, enjoyed pictures with Abby through the recorder, talked about her growing up, the birds and the bees, and if she needed anything or anyone to talk to Alisse was who she should talk to. She would take good care of her and her brother. Ava talked about an hour and closed out with the comfort that she'd always be by her side as her guardian angel.

Ava stopped the recorder, and then looked through Abbie's picture book one more time. *Oh how time flies*, she thought.

Ava took the camcorder and went and sat up in Jaxon's room to do the same thing. She pulled out his picture book, sat in the chair and hit record.

*Jaxon, son, this is for you.* Ava paused and after a brief moment she continued.

*Mom is really sick and has been for awhile. I have ovarian cancer that I've been battling with. My hair is gone, my weight has dropped, and I get weak every day. I didn't tell you guys because I didn't want you to worry. I know you will be okay, you're my big man. I want you and Abbie to always look out for each other.*

Ava paused again holding up pictures to the recorder. She repeated basically what she talked about with Abbie, but if he had boy questions to go to his father. Jaxon was a mama's boy so she didn't know how this would affect him. Ava tried to make both of

*Love and War*

them feel comfortable and not sad. She wrapped up the recorder and blew him a kiss as this is not goodbye, but see you later son.

Ava glanced at Jaxon's photos and smiled. He was her son, brave, and full of life.

Ava's body started to ache as she moved around. She put her wig back on, then took the equipment into the bedroom only to find herself recording again, this time for Ryan. There was so much she had to say and get off her chest. Their life was filled with so much love only to end with so much pain.

Ava got comfortable in the chair then hit record.

*Hello, Ryan I don't know where to start, but I have so much to say. First of all I'm sick; I've been diagnosed with stage 4 ovarian cancer. The surgery I had a couple of months ago, which you thought was just a hysterectomy, was when I first found out about the cancer. After the surgery, it was gone, but has reoccurred and it's not curable; so, I'm dying Ryan. I kept it from the kids because I didn't want to worry them and the same goes for you. When you asked me for a divorce I didn't feel the need to tell you. The cancer has spread to the majority of my organs.*

*Ava took her wig off and held it up to the camcorder. "You see, Ryan, I've been through hell from losing my hair, chemo treatments, radiation, and weight loss while you abandon me for that whore!" I loved you until death!*

Ava paused and cried.

Then Ava got angry about how badly he hurt her, and she tried to forgive him. Ava told him he wasn't getting a dime of her money, she worked too damn hard. He took her off of the insurance policy before they were even divorced; therefore, he wasn't getting a dime!

Ava calmed down, wiped her tears and explained through it all that she still loved him. The only thing she asked was the kids' approval of whomever he decided to marry, be the best father ever, and to take good care of Abbie and Jaxon.

Ava went through their wedding album, held up pictures from the good and bad times and how they were made for each other, never in a million years would she have divorced Ryan. Ava told him she forgives him; he will always have a special place in her heart. Ava blew him a kiss, smiled, and said "I love you, Ryan," then hit stop on the recorder.

Ava didn't hold back tears this time, she let them fall as she gathered the pictures and put them back. Ava's next task was to write each of her girls a letter, and also her mom, Alisse, and Malcolm. She wanted them all to know how much she loved them and to explain to Karen and Lisa why she didn't tell them about the cancer.

Spending the entire morning recording, Ava sat at her desk, writing her thoughts out on a notepad. Ava started with Karen first. She wrote about how it all began. She wrote, then balled up the paper, then wrote again only to break down and cry. Ava sucked it

*Love and War*

up and wrote Karen a five page letter, inserted pictures, then sealed it with her initials. She then continued with Lisa, Angela, Alisse, her mom, and then Malcolm. Writing and reminiscing took Ava hours, but she would do it again if she had to. Ava took out the gifts and bracelets she had delivered from L.A. and decided they would each get them along with their letter.

    Ava glanced at her phone and noticed two missed calls from Malcolm. Never had she met anyone like him. Ava thought God sent him here to help her deal with her illness because without him she would have been dead months ago. Ava smiled knowing that someone cared.

    Ava took out the letter she wrote to Malcolm only to read it once more. She sealed everyone else's, but his.

    *Dear Malcolm,*

    *How can I thank you enough for being my guardian angel? If only I had more time to show you how much you mean to me. You've been a great friend for only a short period of time, but still I felt I've known you a lifetime. I've grown over the last couple of months because of you; you've made me accept me for me and gave me that desire to love again.*

    *I hope that you find someone just as good as me to love you the way I couldn't. Timing was bad for us here on earth, next lifetime will be better. You will always hold a special place in my heart and because of that I have truly fallen in love with you. If only I had the chance to make love to the one man who put my needs first. Thanks for all the pep talks, date nights, walks in the park and most importantly how to love. You've encourage me to stay strong and fight. Malcolm my battle is over, I've fought a good fight, but did not win this round.*

*Malcolm, I LOVE YOU! This past month has been hell fighting cancer and going through a divorce, but you've helped me through it. I have to go for now; I'll see you on the other side. I'll wait for you as long as you wait for me.*

*P.S: Keep being that wonderful soul that you are. You're going to make a great husband and father to a very lucky lady☺.*

*Love,*

*Ava Decree, aka Your Sugafoot*

Ava folded the letter back, placed it back in the envelope and included a picture of them taken at his place, which she had developed. Ava placed the necklace Malcolm bought her for Mother's Day inside the envelope as well, and then sealed it with a kiss.

Ava thought when bad things happen like an illness, life is looked at, at a whole other angle. Things that once mattered began to fade into the things that do matter.

*Love and War*

## **Through the Good and the Bad**

**R**yan's mind has been on Ava for the last couple of days. He noticed she's been spending more time with the kids and more evenings away from home. Ryan knows she just completed another book, which has been keeping her busy plus her movie is due out soon. He was so proud of her.

The divorce was getting close, and they still haven't told the kids. Not sure if he was having second thoughts, but as he carried Ava down the stairs that morning he smelled the fragrance on her blouse then realized he hadn't looked at Ava carefully for a long time. When she wrapped her arms around his neck, Ryan felt a sense of intimacy returning. The last couple of days have made him feel some type of way, even the kids got excited when it was time to carry Ava downstairs.

Ryan wanted to call Ava, his wife, to tell her how much he loves her, but felt something holding him back.

Sharon and Ryan were finally getting back on track after the incident that happened at her place. When he questioned Sharon about dining with Ricky she explained he's someone she could talk to, so she called him to talk about some things, including Tiffany's dad. Ryan didn't buy it at first, until he met Ricky's fiancée. Sharon insisted Ryan stop listening to everyone and trust her; she even offered to give the account to someone else if it made him feel any better, that way she wouldn't have to deal with Ryan or Ricky.

Ryan apologized for his actions so that they could move forward. For some reason he felt torn between letting Ava go and moving on with Sharon.

He looked up only to find Andrew standing at his desk.

"I guess people don't knock these days," Ryan said.

"I did knock, but somebody was off in space," Andrew said.

Andrew handed Ryan a folder with contracts to look over and sign off on. Ryan told him it will be awhile before he can get to them. He wasn't making the same mistake he did with Ricky.

"That's cool, I got a lot of work to keep me busy," Andrew said.

Ryan could tell he wanted to ask him something or say more, but he pretended like he was swamped with work. Andrew walked off, then shortly after his phone rang.

*Love and War*

The receptionist put Brian through..."Hey, man, how's it going?" he said.

"It's going, work that's about all. I got up with Brent last night, he asked about you," Brian said

"Word...man, we got to get together soon I've been busy. You know my situation and it's not getting any easier," Ryan said.

Ryan put Brian on speaker, got up and closed his door. There was no telling who was listening.

"Well, you know what I say, it's cheaper to keep her. On the real Ava has given you thirteen plus years of her life; you two have chemistry, man. Life is short, what you have with Sharon won't amount to what you and Ava have. Remember you cheated on her so you brought these problems on yourself. Just because the pussy is good with Sharon, is that enough?" Brian asked getting deep.

Ryan understood what Brian was saying, but no one knew Ava or Sharon better than he did.

"I hear you, man. I've been here thinking whether I'm making the right decision," Ryan said.

"Are you happy with Ava?" Brian asked.

"Yes. No. I mean...I can't really answer that. I was, and then came Sharon, so my attention turned to her."

"What about Sharon, are you happier with her?" He asked.

"Again, I can't really answer. Brian, what I'm trying to say is I'm happy with Sharon, the sex is amazing, but she's no Ava. I wish Ava had some of the qualities Sharon has and I wish Sharon had some of the qualities Ava has," Ryan said.

"Then you're more screwed than I thought Ryan, those are things you can correct with Ava. I can't tell you what to do, but make sure it's not too late to fix it. Look, I have to go; I have someone at my door. We'll get together soon," Brian said.

Ryan thought about what Brian said, but he needed more. Ava was his past and Sharon was his future. Everything was in place with the divorce less than thirty days it'll all be over.

Ryan sat there trying to convince himself over and over again that he was making the right decision, but deep down he was having second thoughts.

*Love and War*

## ***Putting Everything into Perspective***

$A$va finally put the finishing touches on her memoir. She clicked the send button on her laptop and forwarded the completed manuscript to her editor. Ava created a to-do list to help her prepare for whatever it was ahead and checked off on her next task.

Ava visited Jehovah Shalom Gardens yesterday, where she met with Pastor Boeing as she prepared to put together her own memorial service, including her eulogy. Ava made the decision to be cremated after her close family and friends viewed her one last time if they decided to do so. She wanted her ashes to be spread around Lake Vale. Ava left special instructions with her pastor, who would see to it that everything went according to her plan. Doing things this way made everything as simple as possible for her love ones.

Ava even had her will notarized and all banking information put in place, but the one thing she had left to do on her list, which she avoided, was Malcolm. Malcolm had called and left messages; he even reached out to Angela.

Ava cared for him so much that she decided he deserved better. Ava was near death and her being around him only made it worse. She ended up befriending Malcolm just to get her mind off of Ryan and his infidelities, but ended up caring for and loving a man she couldn't be with.

As Ava stood in the mirror and looked at her aging body, she noticed she was getting thinner and thinner. Ava had no appetite, stopped chemo altogether, vomited every day, and her pain was getting worse. The only thing Dr. Patel would give her was morphine.

Elaine came over every morning after Ryan and the kids left. She also had a nurse check in every other morning to get her blood count. Ava felt fatigued, but managed to get around. Ava heard noise downstairs and instantly pulled her shirt down and threw on her wig.

"Baby, you have company downstairs," mom called out.

"Who is it?" Ava yelled.

"Malcolm," Ava heard a male voice say. She knew that voice anywhere.

She thought to herself, *What is this man doing in my home? If Ryan came home, he would have a fit*. But the thought of him coming to see her made her smile.

*Love and War*

Ava slowly walked down the steps only to find Malcolm waiting for her at the bottom of the stairs.

"What a surprise," she said.

"I'll leave you two alone. Going to pick up your meds, Ava," Elaine said.

They both returned a smile to one another, as Ava lead Malcolm to the sitting area. He looked around, picked up photos, admired her safari collection, and then stared at a photo of her during happier times.

"Nice home, Ava," Malcolm said taking a seat right beside her.

"Thank you! You look great," Ava said turning to him. "It's been awhile."

"Yes, it has and I've been worried about you. I know you've got all my messages and texts, what's going on?" Malcolm asked.

"Malcolm, I'm sorry, I did plan on contacting you today," she said as he looked at her like she was lying. "I've been trying to get everything in order on my end, I've gotten sicker, and honestly, I think you deserve better."

Malcolm took Ava's hand, brought her close, and then looked her in the eyes.

"Ava, let me decide what I deserve; your well-being has become my concern. I took a chance coming to your home, a place you share with your husband....that means I care."

Ava just knew he would find the right words to say. She embraced him and promised to stay in touch. He asked how she was doing, how she was feeling, what her doctors were saying, the aches and pains, as well as how she's eating.

Malcolm took Ava's feet and massaged them as they talked. Ava touched briefly on how she and Ryan were doing in terms of the divorce and how they were still moving forward with it. She also told him that she had not told Ryan about the cancer.

Although Malcolm thought Ava should tell him, he also understood why she was keeping it from him. Malcolm then started massaging her shoulders and promised to always be there for her. Malcolm helped Ava from the couch as he heard her mom's car pull in the driveway; she immediately fell in his arms. Ava found Malcolm's lips and kissed him deeply. She pulled back and gazed in his eyes.

"Malcolm, the one thing I want to do when I get well is make love to you; that is, after the divorce," she said smiling.

"I'm holding you to your word, princess," Malcolm smiled.

Elaine came in as Ava was walking Malcolm to the door.

"Malcolm, wait I got something for you," Ava said. "Mom, can you go get that box beside the bed."

Ava playfully joked with Malcolm, who pulled her hair out of her face only to kiss her again.

"Here you go, baby," Elaine said as she handed Ava the wrapped box.

*Love and War*

"Malcolm, this is for you. I wrapped it especially for you. Promise me you won't open it. I mean, this is a keepsake only if something happens; you know, if God decides to come for me." Ava said.

She gave him the gift wrapped box, he shook it, "Ava, I don't know what to say. I want you to live life. God's plan is that, His plan. If something happens I'll be there to catch you," he said winking at Ava. "Besides I won't have a reason to open this."

They said their goodbyes as Ava whispered to Malcolm, "I love you."

As soon as she closed the door Elaine was standing right behind her.

"Mom, please don't judge me," Ava said as she slowly walked back to the couch.

"Baby, I wouldn't dare do that. I look at your situation and all that you're dealing with, I really admire you, Ava. I wished you could have met Malcolm earlier though, he's a nice guy," Elaine said.

"Yeah, he really is. He came into my life at my worst, Mom. I don't understand."

"Baby girl, it's not for you to understand; it's all part of God's plans. It's called fate!"

Elaine took off Ava's wig then massaged her head. Ava was glad to know that her mom would be okay if something ever happened to her. She was also glad that her kids would have a good support team besides Ryan. Family was everything to Ava, which was the reason she kept holding on to Ryan.

*Love and War*

## *One Week Later...*

*I*t was Ava's 40th birthday and Angela was excited to get all the girls together with a slew of business associates, family, and friends for a celebration at Ava's place. Ava wasn't in the mood for a grand celebration and, since she wasn't at her best, Angela put her differences aside with Ryan and talked him into having the dinner celebration at their place, under the condition that she wouldn't say anything negative about him since this was about Ava.

    Ava was getting weaker day by day, although Ryan didn't know what was going on, he knew something was wrong with her. Ava didn't want a celebration, but Alisse talked her into it and promised it would be short and sweet.

    Angela had someone go by Ava's and take her a couple of designs to wear for the evening and someone to do her make-up and hair, so she wouldn't feel or look uncomfortable in front of everyone. Although Angela didn't want to admit it, she just had a feeling this would be their last gathering together, so she wanted to make it special.

Karen called Angela last night and begged her to tell her what's going on with Ava. When Karen phoned Ava she stated she was talking out of her mind. Angela almost blurted it out, but she had to catch herself, she wanted so desperately to tell Karen and Lisa.

Angela told herself that she was at peace if the Lord takes her, but you could never prepare yourself for death.

Time was ticking. Angela had to hurry and pick up the balloons, cake, and the canvas she had painted for Ava. Angela and the girls thought it would be a perfect gift for the occasion. Although Ryan didn't want to be involved he's been very helpful where Ava is concern, even she knew it's too late for that.

"Babe, where are you headed to?" Carl asked walking into the bedroom, noticing Angela putting on her shoes.

"I'm going to pick up a few things for Ava's party," she replied.

"You wearing that?" Carl replied looking at her get-up gear.

"No silly, I'm taking clothes and will change before the party. What time will you be arriving?"

"I'll be there. Babe, what's going on with Ava? She looked sick the last time we stopped by. I didn't want to say anything, but

## Love and War

something ain't right, Angela," Carl asked Angela waiting on a response.

Right there at that moment she could have broken down. Angela wanted to tell Carl so badly, but couldn't.

"Baby, she is, I can't say. Remember? I'm sworn to secrecy, but I promise you in due time."

"Angela, is she dying? Does Ryan know?" Carl kept pushing.

Angela didn't say anything, but grabbed her bag containing her change of clothes, and make-up bag then headed downstairs with Carl right behind her.

"Angela, answer me!" he said grabbing her arm.

"Carl, not right now, we'll talk about it later!" she said.

"I'm calling Ryan to see what he knows!"

"No! Okay, Carl! She has cancer and she's dying! Baby, my best friend is dying and I can't do nothing about it. That's why I want to make her birthday party so special. It may be our last time together. That's why I've being spending so much time with her!" Angela hollered and balled up crying like a baby.

Carl got down on the floor where Angela was and held her. "Baby, I'm sorry, I had no idea. I'm so, so sorry," he said.

"Promise me you won't say anything. No one really knows, Carl, that's why I promised to keep the secret. Ryan doesn't even know, it's not like he cares; he's divorcing her!"

"I promise, Angela, but I do feel like he should know. Besides I think he's having second thoughts about the divorce," Carl said.

Angela got herself together and wiped her face, "It doesn't matter the damage has already been done," she said.

Angela headed out the door, running right into the sun, which blinded her as usual. Carl stared at her, Angela looked back thinking he was going to say something, but he just blew her a kiss and stood there until she drove off.

This was one time Angela hopes he keeps his mouth shut. Carl is not a talker when it comes to other people's business, but in this case it's different and he has heart, but she prayed it wouldn't slip.

---

Angela arrived at Ava's home to find the place decked out. Alisse and Justin did a marvelous job thus far. The theme was "Old Hollywood Glam, Aged to Perfection." The decorations were fabulous and colorful and the backyard was nicely done.

There was the gazebo, tables, chairs, a photo booth, and we had a small bar section where Angela hired a server and a DJ for the evening. Angela put the tier Chanel cakes she had made on the

*Love and War*

table, then spread balloons all over the place. Angela added alcohol to the bar and sanitizer through the area.

Lisa arrived with gourmet cupcakes and things for the chocolate bar she wanted to set up as well as Jonathan on her arm who offered to help. Ryan came in and offered to help as well, not sure what's up with his sudden mood change, but Angela wasn't buying it.

Angela snuck up stairs to check on Ava. She peeped into the room as the make-up artist was putting the finishing touches to her face, Ava looked like the old Ava, and she was stunning.

"You like?" Ava asked

"Hell, yeah! You look amazing, Ava!"

"I chose the Black Kami Shade Sequin gown with the slits on the side. It's doesn't show my skinny legs and arms due to all the shrinkage, like all the other dresses do," Ava said.

"How do you feel?" Angela asked.

"Right now okay, but earlier I was throwing up green stuff. I just need to make it through this party. You know I didn't think I'll make it to see my 40$^{th}$ birthday. Lord, behold, I did," Ava said.

"You'll make it next year, sis." Angela said smiling.

"I want to lie down and take it easy until the party."

"That's fine; I'll come up and get you."

Angela left Ava alone and headed back downstairs. She bumped into Karen who looked bigger by the day. Karen was now

7 1/2 months pregnant with a baby girl, Angela was so happy for her.

They hugged, and then she sat down saying she was tired.

"Where's the birthday girl?" Karen asked.

"She's sleeping, said she'll make a grand entrance," Angela said to everyone lying, this way she can rest with no distractions.

"Angela, you remember Chris, my baby daddy," Karen said as she noticed him sitting on the other side.

"Yes, I do girl, you're too funny. Baby daddy," Angela said shaking her head.

*I could have sworn his name was Bob*, Angela thought. Glad she wasn't drinking there's no telling what she would have called him.

Angela went into the spare room and changed into her Hollywood attire. She asked the make-up artist to stay and fix her up as well. Angela wore an off white back drop shimmery dress with gold pumps. People were starting to arrive so she hurried as Lisa barged in to get her make-up before the lady left.

"Girl, how many people did y'all invite? It's a lot of people on the deck," Lisa said.

Angela laughed at how Lisa talked sometimes; she was business and hood at the same damn time.

"Not many, maybe forty people at the max."

*Love and War*

"It doesn't look like it! I hope the food doesn't get gone, I want to take a plate for later," Lisa said laughing at her own statement. The make-up artist even laughed.

Angela just shook her head. "Girl, let's head down stairs."

Alisse passed Angela and said she was bringing Ava out now, which was cool by Angela.

Angela went out back and mingled with the guests and to make sure everything was on cue. Angela noticed Carl talking to Brian, Ryan's close friend, as she approached him. Moments later they all looked up and saw everyone clapping as Alisse welcomed everyone to Ava's "Hollywood Glam Bash," followed by Ava in a long gorgeous gown. Angela noticed Ryan smiling when Ava walked down the stairway.

Everyone was going up to Ava taking photos as Angela stood there and watched. "You're not going up there?" Carl asked.

"Not now, I want everyone else to have their moment with her," Angela said. Carl grabbed her hand and squeezed it.

The DJ was playing all of Ava's favorite songs; the waiter had hors d'oeuvres and glasses of wine approaching each guest. Angela noticed Ava's publisher, her editor, some of her author friends Alisse invited, co-stars from her movie, friends, and family. She also noticed some of Ryan and Carl co-workers, not sure why they were there at Ava's event since Ryan didn't want anything to do with it at first.

Ava didn't want this to take long, so Angela wanted to try and speed things up. Alisse kicked things off followed by dinner. Angela hoped she could get Ava to mingle a bit, take a couple photos, and get her to talk before she got tired.

Dinner was followed by a toast from Ryan. Everyone that knew about Ryan and Ava was shocked he was even speaking. He's been on his phone all evening, but eye balling Ava. Lisa nudged Angela in the leg when Ryan started to speak.

"I want to wish the mother of my children, the lady who has blessed me with thirteen wonderful years of marriage, a businesswoman, a devoted friend with a loving spirit, a Happy 40th Birthday! Cheers, Ava," Ryan said as everyone took a sip of whatever they had in their glass.

Angela looked at Karen, who asked "What was that all about?" Angela shrugged her shoulders.

Guests were talking, then talking turned to laughter. Elaine, Ava's mom, went to check on her; she was sitting at the table up front. Angela saw a nice looking gentleman stand up to propose another toast and realized it was Malcolm.

"What the hell? What's he doing here?" she mumbled.

"This toast goes to a special lady with a loving heart. I met Ava months ago and her spirit is the same as it was then. It's good to see everyone that loves her in the same room and that says a lot. I just want to wish you a Happy Birthday, Ava, may it last forever," Malcolm said as he sat down next to Alisse.

*Love and War*

Angela pulled out her phone and texted her quick!

*MSG: What's Malcolm doing here?*

Angela heard Ryan ask who that guy was. The look on Lisa's face almost gave away who he was, she was glad Ava found someone else.

*Alisse: MSG: I invited him; I thought he should be here* ☺

The waiter brought the cake out as Alisse helped Ava up to stand. They all sang happy birthday as Ava managed to blow out the candles. Ryan walked over to Ava and presented her with a tiny box. Ava looked surprise as she told him she'll open it later. Ryan walked off as Ava cut the cake and handed everyone a piece. Malcolm walked over to speak with Ava; he playfully dotted her nose with frosting. Ryan looked on in disbelief still trying to figure out who the guy was. Malcolm stated he was leaving and left something for Ava with Alisse.

"I hope you like them," Malcolm said giving Ava a hug before leaving.

"Them?"

"You'll like, I guarantee it," he said.

"Thank you for coming, it's always good to see you," Ava said as she smiled then turned her attention to Angela, Lisa, Alissa, and Karen. Lisa presented her with the canvas they had made and she just loved it. It was a photo Ava took in Cancun that Angela just fell in love with; Ava had no worries at that moment. Ava was banging and Angela wanted her to remember that.

Everyone was in awe of the canvas. Ryan just stood back and looked on. Chris held on to Karen as she gave a speech on how she and Ava met, then the celebration turned into something emotional from Lisa, Angela, Ava's agent, Elaine, and most of all, Ava's kids. Alisse had them to come out for a brief moment to present their mom with a rose for each year of her life. Ava knew she was loved; she gave a heartfelt speech to everyone and thanked them for coming.

"I don't want to get sentimental, but I appreciate everyone here and those who have made this day so special. To my lovely kids, family, friends, business partners, I love you all! Now, let's party!" Ava said.

Angela could tell Ryan felt some kind of way because nowhere in Ava's speech did she mention her husband, he just stood off in the cut.

The kids went back in, the DJ started spinning, and everyone had a good time. People were dancing, drinking, mingling, and taking pictures in the photo booth; what they had put in place was more than Ava asked for, but Angela could tell Ava was getting tired of this battle.

"Angela, come on," Lisa called out for her to join them at the photo booth.

They took about ten photos from Hollywood Glam to showing how silly they could be.

"Karen, you got to move that big belly," Ava said.

*Love and War*

"No, I'm just going to turn the other way, so my belly won't be in the way," Karen said.

After taking photos Ava went over and touched Karen's belly talking to the baby, she was saying things that had Karen puzzled like, "Auntie hopes she be around to meet this princess," "I know you're going to be gorgeous," and "also Auntie left you something." At that moment Karen wanted to question Ava regarding her comments but opted out.

Elaine walked over for Ava to sit. Angela motioned for the girls beside Karen to start cleaning up, so people could go home. Carl stopped Angela and pulled her out onto the dance floor, they did the Cupid shuffle, then the wobble came on, and all the ladies went crazy. After dancing and having a good time, Angela looked around for Ava who disappeared into the night. Angela managed to have a good time, but was concerned about Ava.

Angela left the scene and went into the house looking for Ava, where she noticed Elaine crying in the doorway.

"What's going on?" Angela asked.

"Ava started vomiting so we brought her in, now her breathing sounds awful, she's saying things that don't make sense. Angela, I'm scared!" Elaine said.

"Have you called her doctor?"

"No, she doesn't want a doctor, she's knows Angela. No doctor, hospice, she just wants to be at home," Elaine said.

Angela started to go in the room, but Alisse stopped her. Angela respected Alisse's wishes to let them all be in peace. Angela turned around only to bump into Carl. Looking directly in Angela's eyes, he demanded that she tells Ryan.

"No, Carl, not right now," Angela said.

"I'm giving you twenty-four hours Angela, if you don't, then you leave me with no choice!" Carl said as he stormed off.

Angela didn't know what to do, she wanted to go get the girls and tell them of Ava's illness, instead she sat on the stairway with her head in her lap.

*Love and War*

## *When the Heart Speaks*

**R**yan tossed and turned; then he finally got up and cooked breakfast. Ryan noticed the kids were still sleeping so he woke them to join him at church. Ryan hasn't been to church in a while; when Pastor Boeing sees him, he may throw the Bible in his direction.

Ryan peeped in on Ava and noticed Alisse and Elaine by her side wondering what the hell was going on and why they stayed the night.

Ryan went over and shook Ava who moaned at him. Elaine jumped up, "Ryan, what are you doing here?" she asked.

Ryan looked around the room then back at her, "I live here. Remember?"

Alisse got up, shook Ava, and asked if she was okay.

"What's going on? Is Ava sick?" Ryan asked.

"No, she doesn't want to be alone Ryan," Alisse snapped.

"Let me speak to my wife! In private," he said.

"Now she's your wife? Remember your divorce is almost final," Elaine said motioning for Alisse to give them some space. Ryan was so ashamed at Elaine's comment, but it wasn't anything but the truth; he did ask Ava for a divorce, that wasn't a secret.

Ryan sat, and rubbed Ava's head. Ryan noticed the tiny box he gave her for her birthday wasn't opened. Ryan picked up the tiny black box and opened it for her. Ava looked distressed and tired, not saying much. Ryan pulled Ava's wedding ring out of the box. He had it redesigned and told her she was his until death do they apart.

Ryan placed the ring back on her finger where it belonged, only for it to fall right off. Noticing how tiny Ava's hands had become it suddenly hit him how much pain and bitterness she had buried in her heart.

Ryan saw a tear roll down Ava's face; he wiped her face, then promised to give her some time to think about them being together as husband and wife again. He would have it resized for her. Ryan left in a state of shock; he was not sure what he was doing at that moment, that's why he needed to go to church. Then he would go see Sharon afterwards.

The kids were downstairs eating and fully dressed. Ryan went to get himself together and passed Alisse along the way, who looked like she had a long night.

*Love and War*

Ryan hurried so he could be on time for the 10:00 a.m. service. The kids couldn't believe he wanted to go to church, especially Jaxon.

"Dad, it's been a long time since you stepped foot in the house of The Lord."

Abbie chuckled at Jaxon's comment; Ryan slapped Jaxon upside the head playfully and told him to come on.

"Dad, I wish Mom was coming with us," Abbie said.

"I know, sweetheart, she's tired from the party," Ryan said lying. Not sure what was going on with Ava, but he planned to make it better.

Ryan drove until he found himself in Salem Baptist Church parking lot. The kids came to church often; Elaine would bring them or Ava would. Ryan was nervous, but walked anxiously to the door. The usher opened the door and he could have fallen to his knees with all the stares. Ryan found a section in the middle of the church for him and the kids to sit.

It was stuffy and he felt confined between all the people on the pew. The choir started singing a hymn then it turned into one of those Fantasia Burrino breakdowns. The lady singing looked familiar. Ryan watched her dance and shout with no shoes on, then he realized that was Ricky's fiancée. Ryan looked around the church looking for him, but didn't see him. Moments later he saw a smooth looking guy over in the corner ushering and it was Ricky. "When did he become a member?" Ryan wondered. They both made eye contact and Ryan quickly turned his head, Ryan didn't care for him one bit!

The order of service presumed, one of the Deacon's read the scripture, then they took up a collection which lead to prayer. When Pastor Boeing asked those in need of prayer to come to the altar, Ryan looked at his kids and stood up. They both followed him as they stood in line for prayer. Sweat was running on his forehead and Ricky stared at him. Ryan found himself face to face with the Pastor.

"Welcome back, Ryan, glad to have you in the house of The Lord," Pastor Boeing said laying hands on him.

Pastor Boeing began to pray over Ryan without him asking if there was anything he would like for him to pray for. He did the same thing to Abbie and Jaxon as well as the other members standing in line. Finally Pastor Boeing began his sermon and all Ryan could say was, "Boy, is he on fire!"

"Please church turn your bibles to *James 4:7*. I want to touch a little on sinners, deceivers, temptation, and the desire to sin as all is forgiven when we submit ourselves to the King himself. And the scripture reads: *"Submit yourself therefore to God. Resist the devil, and he will flee from you."*

The Pastor preached and although the sermon spoke directly to Ryan, he couldn't help but think about what he put Ava through. Every time Ryan looked up he made eye contact with

*Love and War*

Ricky, who he knew would run straight to Sharon and tell her that he saw him at church.

After service, Ryan hurried out of the church before anyone stopped him. The kids wanted food so they all stopped at a burger joint, grabbed some take out, and then headed home.

Once home, Ryan noticed Elaine was still there and Alisse was gone. Elaine was fixing a pot of soup. Ryan wanted to ask why she was still there, but didn't want to start a big fuss. He went in to see Ava, but the kids got to her first. She was still lounging around. He spoke, but she was too busy listening to Abbie talk about church. Ryan figured he would let them have their moment and he'll have his later, but one thing he needed to do was go see Sharon.

Ryan quickly changed, texted Sharon, and told her he'll be right over to talk, then headed out. Elaine didn't say one word to Ryan. He guessed if his son-in law was cheating on his daughter and the whole town knew, then he would give the man the cold shoulder, too, but he was going to make it right once and for all.

Ryan drove honking his horn at the neighbors down the street. He put his Maze featuring Frankie Beverly CD in the changer and headed south. Listening to "Joy and Pain" took Ryan to a whole other place. After twenty minutes of driving, Ryan noticed a couple of cars at Sharon's condo, Ryan didn't want to get out because he didn't want to engage himself with people or her family and friends at that moment.

Ryan finally got out after sitting in the car briefly waiting on people to come out, but no one left. He wished Sharon would have told him she had company, then again Sharon loved attention. Ryan rang the doorbell, then realized she had given him a key. He placed his key in the lock to open the door, and instead someone opened it for him…and that person had to be Ricky. "What the hell! Not again!" Ryan thought.

Sharon met Ryan at the door, "Hey, baby," she said pecking him on the cheek.

"Hi, sweetheart," he said, eyeing a couple people in the living room area. At that moment Ryan wanted to leave.

Sharon introduced Ryan to her friend, Rhonda, and her spouse, Ricky's fiancée, Sherry, who was hooting and hollering in the choir stand and her aunt Rose. They all were "just stopping by," which just happened to be at the same time.

"Hey, I saw you at church today," the Choir lady, Ricky's fiancée, Sherry, said.

"You were at church today and didn't take me?" Sharon said with her arms folded.

"Yes and yes," Ryan said to both Sherry and Sharon.

"It was good to see you there," Ricky said trying to act sincere.

"Yeah," Ryan said brushing him off. Ryan didn't care for Ricky and this friendship with Sharon and now his fiancée, Sherry, had him on edge.

*Love and War*

"Well, I guess we'll be going," Rhonda said, and then everyone else chimed in to leave as well.

Ryan sat on the couch looking around, waiting on Sharon to come back in from walking everyone out. Ryan didn't know how he was going to do this and explain to Sharon that he felt the need to stay with Ava, but what should he say?

Sharon came back in and his heart started pounding as she sat next to him on the couch.

"So you went to church this morning, huh?"

"Yes, the kids and I did; it felt good. I haven't been in a while. I'm surprised Ricky didn't tell you I was there and when did he start going to church?" Ryan asked.

"No, he didn't mention it. He's being going for a while now, that's how long you've been away I suppose. My Aunt Rose stopped by and brought dinner from Popeye's Chicken and I was surprised to see everyone else stop by," she said.

"Where's Tiffany?" Ryan asked.

"With her father, who just happened to be in town and decided to take her for the weekend, she'll be home later."

Ryan was playing with his hands; her baby daddy was something they rarely discussed since he stayed miles away. Sharon noticed Ryan in deep thought.

"Baby, we need to talk," he blurted out.

"I agree, we do…you go first," she said.

"Ladies first," Ryan said.

Sharon got up to grab her purse off the coffee table. She pulled out a zip lock bag containing a couple sticks she pulled one out and handed it to Ryan.

"What's this?" he said knowing what the hell it was.

"What it looks like. I took all eight of them…a pregnancy test, stupid."

Lord have mercy, Ryan's heart dropped!

"You're pregnant? I thought you had that five year thing inserted?" Ryan said trying to understand. He didn't want a baby.

"Yes, but it's not 100% guaranteed; besides I'm excited. Ryan, I love you. Besides your divorce is almost final and it's the right time," Sharon said.

For some reason Ryan couldn't help but think this was a set up to keep him. Lord behold she's going to flip when he tell her about Ava, right now that was on the back burner.

"Sharon, I don't know what to say. I think it's too soon, meaning the ink is not on the divorce papers yet!"

"But it will be," she said catching an attitude.

Ryan wiped the sweat from his face and looked at her. Sharon rubbed his face and smiled as if he was supposed to be happy. Ryan was really lost for words trying to think of ways for her to get rid of the baby. Ryan loved Sharon, but wanted to stay with Ava. After giving his situation some serious thought, he would like a baby only if it was done right, and this was all wrong!

*Love and War*

Sharon stood up, took Ryan by the hand and he knew what she wanted. It's always sex with her, which is really good, but it's getting old. A man needs more.

Ryan followed her lead, went into the bedroom and undressed just for the hell of it. He figured he'll make love to her this one last time and tell her the news about Ava tomorrow.

"Love making is good for the baby, you know," Sharon said taking Ryan hand and rubbing it against her stomach.

"Who else knows about the baby?"

"No one. Although I wanted to tell Aunt Rose; she said I had this glow about myself."

One thing for sure Ricky didn't need to know about this.

Ryan motioned for Sharon to get on his dick, which was at attention as he stroked himself for her to do her job. Sharon crawled on the bed like a tiger and took over. She took his balls in her mouth, licked his shaft, and then took his dick in her mouth and slobbed Ryan down.

Sharon's warm mouth felt good on his wood; she could be another "super head," she did her job well.

"Baby, you sucking the venom out of me," Ryan said moaning and groaning trying not to cum.

"I want to suck you dry! Cum, baby, cum..."

"I don't want to; not right now," he managed to say.

"Cum in my mouth, I want to taste you," she said.

"Aww damn damn damn, its coming. Open your mouth, Sharon...open it! I want you to suck it all out," Ryan said.

The way Sharon sucked him and played with his balls at the same time left Ryan empty. He busted one good nut in her mouth, some managed to get in her hair.

After that, she straddled Ryan, then glided up and down. He bounced her around, played with her clit, then flipped her over to eat her out. Ryan wanted Sharon to skeet like a water hose. He found her spot, then all he heard was "Ryan, I love you!"

Sharon held her ass up as he felt her exploding. She came as he thought she would – like a water hose. Ryan got on top of Sharon and made love to her like it was their last time.

After their make out session, Ryan held Sharon and admired her body, it was flawless. She had it all ass, tits, flat stomach, no cellulite, just nice to look at; but her personality was what attracted him to her. Ryan really fell for what he saw and after talking to Brian he did some serious thinking and soul searching.

"A penny for your thoughts? Ryan, you made love to me like never before," Sharon said.

Ryan shrugged his shoulders and continued to play with her hair. He wanted to tell her the truth at that moment, but couldn't bring himself to it.

The baby news played in his mind over and over again, his kids wouldn't accept that child.

*Love and War*

    *It's over*, he thought when he left Sharon's place. Ryan couldn't keep hurting Ava; she deserved better. He promised after today, he was going to make it right and get his wife back.

*Bianca Harrison*

## *Timing is Everything*

$A$va's illness was weighing heavily on Carl. After he noticed how sick she really was, he demanded that Angela tell Ryan first thing tomorrow or he would.

*I should not have told Carl,* she thought to herself, *although Ryan wasn't shit these days.* Angela guessed he did need to know since he was Abbie and Jaxon's father.

Angela wasn't being selfish; she's just respecting Ava's wishes and hoped Carl would have understood that. Angela went by Ava's earlier and she was in the bed looking out in space. Angela hated seeing her in that state of mind. She wanted to tell the girls so badly it was killing her inside, so now she understood Carl and why he felt Ryan should know.

Angela promised to stop by the office and tell Ryan in person, then call the girls and tell them as well, she just hoped Ava understood her reasoning. Angela just didn't want Lisa to get all bent out of shape like she usually did when something terrible took

*Love and War*

place. Karen was the same way, but she's much calmer than Lisa; she would worry her ass off.

Angela went to the bar for a night cap, she needed a drink. Before she could pour it she heard Christina call out for her.

"Yes, Chrissy," Angela yelled.

"Good night, Mom," she hollered from upstairs.

"Good night, baby. Don't forget to say your prayers and I love you," she responded.

"Love you back," she said.

Angela took one shot after another, left the glass on the bar then headed to bed. She usually didn't drink like that unless something was bothering her or if she just wanted to get wasted.

When Angela walked into the bedroom, Carl was still up. She didn't say anything; just threw her robe on the couch and climbed in bed.

"So, you're not talking to me?" Carl asked.

"I'm good; just don't have anything to say."

"Angela, I just think we need to tell Ryan about Ava before it's too late," Carl said.

"I agree."

Angela finally got comfortable in the bed. Carl reached his arm out for Angela so that she could lay her head down on his shoulders. Between work and Ava, Angela didn't know if she was coming or going.

"Babe, do you think Ava can beat this battle and do the kids know what's going on?" Carl asked.

Angela turned her head towards Carl and looked at him, "To answer your questions, no and no."

Carl looked stunned after Angela answered his question. If Ava made it through, it would be a miracle. Angela saw her test results; she was there at her doctor visit. It was going to take a miracle.

"I'm sorry, Angela, I know Ava's your best friend and I hate she's going through this alone, as well as dealing with a divorce," Carl said.

"She's not alone, Carl, she has great support. She doesn't want the kids worrying and Ryan…well, his priorities are elsewhere these days," Angela said.

They both watched the news a bit then off the lights went. Angela was exhausted and needed some rest. Angela didn't doze off like she thought, so she got up to take a Tylenol PM. After about forty-five minutes of fighting sleep, Angela was finally out for the count.

*Love and War*

## *The Journey*

*A*va couldn't move, she had a hard time trying to come to grip with reality. Jaxon came into the room followed by Abbie, and she hugged her kids for dear life.

Ava rubbed both of their heads as she was waiting for Abbie to holler, "Mom, you're messing my hair up," but she didn't. Instead they both hugged her as if she needed it.

"I love you guys, you hear? I'll always be here for you guys no matter what. Take care of each other," Ava managed to say between slurs and feeling dizzy.

The kids looked at Ava in turmoil trying to figure out what was going on with her, and then Ryan came in without a word and swooped Ava up. Abbie and Jaxon stayed back not knowing what to say. Ava wrapped her arms around Ryan's neck only to be weak as her arms couldn't come to grip.

"You okay, baby?" Ryan asked.

Ava gave a smile; he continued and whispered in her ear, "Ava, I never stopped loving you."

The kids finally followed then clapped when they reached the front entrance. To them, seeing their father carrying their mother out every morning had become an essential part of their lives.

Ava gestured for the kids to come closer and hugged them tightly; again they were quiet, but hugged Ava back for dear life.

The horn blew outside, Ava released the kids and told them that she loved them and always would.

"We love you, too, Mom," Jaxon and Abbie said.

Ava heard them walking down the hall, especially Jaxon, "What's up with Mom?" And Abbie, "I don't know, but I'm worried," she said as they grabbed their back packs and headed out the door.

Ryan sat Ava on the couch then spoke, "Ava, carrying you each day, I realized now that our lives lacked intimacy. I've fallen back in love with you. I love you so much and hope you still feel the same way," he said. Ryan touched Ava's face and continued, "I'm so sorry for what I've put you through, sweetheart. I realized the mistake I was making; now I want to make it right. Ava, I don't want a divorce, I want you."

Ava tried lifting her arms up to caress Ryan's face, but her weakness kept it numb. Ryan got up, then looked back at Ava, "I'll be back shortly, there's something I have to do. Promise me you'll be here when I get back?" he asked.

Ava just gave a warm smile, as Ryan proceeded to leave. Alisse came in right behind him.

---

Ryan drove to the office to pick up a couple of files, so that he could work from home and spend the day with Ava. On the way, all of a sudden, he took a detour heading over to Sharon's place. Ryan called Sharon asking her to stay put until he got there. He ignored all calls as he noticed Carl was trying to get in touch with him. Ryan called his attorney and told him not to file or sign off on the divorce documents, which was to be finalized that day.

Driving, Ryan realized he loved his wife more than ever, she didn't fight him on the divorce, and all she wanted was for him to be happy whether it was with her or Sharon. Ryan became sad as he noticed how much weight Ava had lost because of him, and how much she sacrificed during that difficult time.

If anyone loved hard, it was Ava. One thing Ryan knew was that Sharon couldn't compare to Ava. What he and Ava had was solid, until he decided his marriage wasn't good enough. Ryan hoped he could get back what he once had – his life with Ava and the kids.

Ryan pulled into Sharon's driveway to her condo, jumped out of the car, leaving it running, unlocked. He ran to the door as his heart beat swiftly. Sharon opened the door.

"Ryan, what is it?" Sharon asked.

"Sorry, Sharon I wanted to tell you this yesterday, but I'm not going through with the divorce. I love Ava too much to let her go, I'm so sorry!" he managed to get out.

"Come again?" Sharon said reaching over touching his forehead, "Ryan, do you have a fever? I'm pregnant remember, stop with the foolishness," she said.

Ryan moved her hand off his forehead, "Sharon, carrying Ava each day made me value my marriage. My marriage was boring because I made it boring. Sharon, I am supposed to hold and love Ava until death. I'm sorry, but I won't divorce her."

Sharon went across Ryan's head, then slapped him in the face as he grabbed both of her arms to keep her from hitting him, "You bastard! You've been playing me all this time knowing you weren't going to divorce her! What a coward!" Sharon yelled. She called Ryan names, and told him that she hated him.

Ryan tried to push Sharon into her condo as she got louder and louder. "Ryan, you're going to get what you deserve! You can't go around hurting people and, as for the baby, stay out of our lives!" She said then slammed the door.

Ryan walked to his car only to look back. He felt very badly, his intentions were to never hurt anyone. Ryan jumped in

## Love and War

his car, headed to the nearest floral shop to order a bouquet of flowers for his wife.

"What would you like for me to write on the card, Mr. Decree?" The florist asked.

"I'll carry you out every morning, each day of the week, any time of day, until death do us part," Ryan said smiling.

Ryan text Ava, *MSG: "I stopped the divorce; I love you too much, until death do us apart. I love you, Ava, Ryan"*

Ryan stood there waiting on a response, but nothing. He left the floral shop, and then stopped at the jewelry store to pick up Ava's ring, which he had resized. Ryan wanted to ask Ava to marry him again and renew their vows, he then left the store only to look at his phone thinking it was Ava, but a text from Carl.

MSG: *"911-911-911 please call me."*

Not knowing what that was about, Ryan got in his car and dialed Carl as he then saw Angela calling on the other line, but he ignored her call.

"Hey, man, everything good? I mean what's with the 911 text?" Ryan asked.

"No man, Ava has been keeping something from you. I just found out and thought as a friend you needed to know as well," Carl said.

"What is it?" Ryan yelled.

"Ryan, Ava has terminal ovarian cancer. She's been battling it for months. She didn't want you or the kids to know, so that you all wouldn't worry," he said.

"What! Who told you Angela? So my wife is sick? Is that what you're telling me?" Ryan asked Carl trying to make sense of what he was saying.

"Yes, man, I'm sorry, Ava is dying. With the divorce and her illness, she decided it would be best not to say anything," Carl said.

Ryan was so angry with himself; he just hung up the phone. Carl called back several times, but Ryan didn't pick up. He hurried out the parking lot heading home to comfort Ava.

---

On the other hand, Ava's organs were shutting down and she knew it. Ava tried texting her girls, "I love you" after several failed attempts, she thought the text went through.

Alisse walked into the room and noticed Ava trying to text, then started reaching into the air as if someone was there.

"What is it, Ava?" Alisse asked running to Ava's side.

Alisse knew there was only a matter of time before Ava left her. Alisse had already called Ava's doctor, who was calling in hospice. Alisse did all she could to make sure Ava was comfortable.

Alisse read the text Ryan sent and shook her head. She wanted to call him so badly, but was so angry at how he treated Ava.

"Text Ryan, Lisse" Ava slurred. "Tell him I love him, too."

Alisse texted her mom to hurry over, then Ryan as Ava asked her to. Alisse noticed a text from Karen *Love you more!! Ava, are you okay?*

Alisse watched Ava, who was confused about where she was, started asking for Grandpa who had been dead for a decade. Then she seemed to come back to reality as she went in and out.

"Lisssee water," Ava got out as her breathing became noisy.

Alisse squeezed Ava's hand, kissed her on the cheek, and said, "I love you, sister."

Alisse then left the room to get water as Elaine banged on the door. Alisse let her in as she filled Ava's cup with water. They both headed to the bedroom only to find Ava unconscious. Elaine ran to Ava's side as the cup fell from Alisse's hands, Alisse just stood there she knew Ava sent her out the room so she could die in peace.

"No, Ava, baby, wake up!" Elaine kept hollering trying to find a pulse.

Alisse knew Ava was gone…she was tired.

"Don't just stand there, do something!" Elaine said yelling at Alisse.

Alisse ran over to help Elaine bring Ava back…"Ava, wake up! Please come back to us," Alisse then put her arms around Ava trying to lift her.

Alisse heard Ryan call out downstairs, as he ran upstairs holding a bouquet of flowers calling out for Ava, he ran over to Ava noticing her stiffness and all the commotion.

"Ava NOOOO….sweetheart, wake up," Ryan called out while trying to shake her to open her eyes. "Baby, I need you to wake up, I need you, Ava! Baby, I'm sorry, please wake up!" Ryan began to holler.

Ryan looked at Alisse, "Why didn't you tell me, dammit? Why didn't you?" Ryan hollered, wiping tears from his face.

Ryan kept hollering then started blaming himself, "This is not happening!" he screamed. Ryan fell to his knees in sudden disbelief banging his head on the floor while Ava was lifeless on the bed.

*Love and War*

## **Too Soon**

*A*fter receiving Ava's last text, Angela knew in her heart something was wrong. Angela left work in a hurry calling Karen and Lisa as she drove to Ava's. Lisa and Karen were furious with Angela when they learned of Ava's illness.

    Lisa got so mad that she hung up on Angela. Angela panicked and called Carl just when Alisse beeped in on the other line and gave Angela the news. Angela had to pull over onto the side on the road just to let it all out.

    After minutes of crying, Angela got the strength to drive. She finally made it over to Ava's when Carl met her in the driveway. Angela ran into his arms like a little girl did with her father. They made it into the house when Angela saw Lisa and Karen who beat her there. Lisa cut her eye at Angela like a mad woman.

    Elaine was coming down the stairs and Angela felt nothing but pain for her.

"I'm so sorry, Elaine," Angela said crying.

"Baby, it's okay, Ava is at peace now. No more suffering, she wouldn't want us to cry, now would she, Angela?"

"No," Angela said in between sniffs.

Angela walked over to the girls with Carl right behind her.

"Lisa and Karen, I'm so sorry."

"Save it!" Karen snapped as Lisa looked on in tears.

"Ava told me to keep this from you two because she knew you all would freak out, I had to respect her wishes, as hard as it was," Angela said.

Right then Lisa hugged Angela and Karen joined in.

"We all we got!" Lisa said trying to stay calm.

Alisse walked over, "You all may go see Ava one last time before they take her," she said. They all looked at each other, but didn't budge.

"Come.." Alisse said leading them to Ava's room. As they all walked Angela noticed every picture on the wall, Ava beamed and that made her happy to know she lived.

When they got to the room, Ava's body was propped up in bed as if she was just sleeping. Angela went over and kissed her, "My friend, you will be missed dearly, no one can ever replace you," Angela said as she gently massaged Ava's hand.

Karen was shaking, but she did go over, say a few words, and kissed Ava on the cheeks, Karen then ran out the room in tears. Carl went after Karen to make sure she was okay. Lisa was

*Love and War*

brave; she had her moment, and then she gathered herself together and said her final goodbye. Sad as it was, Angela didn't know what to feel, especially being so close to Ava through her transition.

Elaine called for the girls as Ryan and the kids were coming up. Abbie and Jaxon were a total wreck just learning of their mother's passing was heartbreaking. Lisa went ahead as Angela stayed with Alisse and Elaine to comfort the kids. They took it pretty hard and when they broke down, everyone broke down as well.

"Mom, please come back! Why God....why did you take my mom?" Abbie hollered as she cried hysterically.

Jaxon, on the other hand, climbed in bed with Ava as Ryan and his friend, Brian, tried to get him out, it was way too much to bear. Angela held Abbie when she went over and kissed Ava.

Finally Ryan was not able to control Jaxon, who ran over and kissed Ava, demanding that she wake up. The nurse asked them all to leave as the members of Jehovah Gardens, the funeral home Ava choose, were there to take her away.

As they all stood downstairs, Angela watched Ryan, who also was an emotional wreck, as she went over to pay her respects. Ryan didn't say much, but fell to his knees as Ava's body was wheeled out the door. Alisse had taken the kids into the other room to calm them down, which was right on time.

"Baby, are you okay?" Carl asked.

"No not really, but I'll be okay. Ava wouldn't want me to cry," Angela said. Angela tried hard to fight it; although, they had been through this several times, but the end results are always worse.

Angela went in to talk with the kids. They didn't understand and it would take time for them to accept that Ava was gone. Angela promised to always be there for them. She then went to check on Ryan, who blamed himself and at that moment Angela really felt sorry for him. With all he put Ava through, she made sure he felt her pain. Angela knew it would happen, but wished it was under different circumstances.

Ryan was really lost for words. "Angela, how do I help my kids through this ordeal when I can barely help myself? Huh?" Ryan asked while rubbing his head.

"Carl and I are here for you, Ryan. I made a promise to Ava to watch over you all," she said.

Ryan looked at Angela, "Why, Angela? Why didn't you tell me about my wife's illness?" He asked. "You hated me that much?"

As Angela was about to answer, Alisse cut her off.

"Would it have mattered, Ryan? You were divorcing my sister anyway. You were too busy with your mistress that you didn't even notice Ava was sick, so no one had to tell you anything! Just the day before you were at Sharon's house while my

## Love and War

sister was fighting for her life. This is a small world, Ryan!" Alisse snapped.

Angela gently grabbed Alisse by the hand to get her to walk with her.

"Yeah, I guess I deserve that Alisse, so I'm the bad guy! Regardless I should have known about Ava and not the day of!" Ryan shot back while Alisse was exiting the room and stormed off.

Angela was mentally drained and the chaos wasn't helping. Her main priority was helping the kids and the family deal. Angela walked over to where Karen was sitting rubbing her belly; she was admiring Ava's photo album. Angela took a seat as Lisa came over and flopped down on the couch as well. Angela took each of the girls hand and they immediately embraced each other.

"I'm sure going to miss her…Ava really did know how to light up a room," Angela said.

"Yes she did," Karen added. Karen then took their hands and placed it on her belly for them to feel the baby kick after a brief moment Karen turned towards them, "My princess! I'm naming her Ava," Karen said smiling.

"Aw, that is so sweet of you, Karen. I bet Ava is smiling" Lisa said still rubbing Karen's belly.

"Ava, huh? I like," Angela said smiling. "Ava would really love that, Karen, she would."

As they went through the photo album together they smiled, laughed and even cried a bit remembering Ava's last days at her birthday party and then noticing the canvas she had placed near the fireplace.

*Love and War*

## ***What Really Matters***

*T*he news of Ava's death spread quickly. Given Ava's popularity as author-turned-movie-producer, every news channel had a quick coverage on her life.

The last twenty-four hours were unreal. The kids weren't doing well and Ryan was coping the best he knew how. Never in a million years would he have seen that coming. Ryan should have known something was wrong with Ava due to her sudden weight loss, her actions; overall he should have paid more attention to the signs. Ryan thought they had a second chance together, the only thing he holds is Ava's last text message and what really hurt the most is all the preparation for the funeral had been prepared by Ava herself.

Ryan sat alone thinking about what he had done. The thought of Ava going through that journey alone without him made him sadder than anything he could ever imagine.

Ryan cried all night thinking about Ava, his kids, and most of all his actions over the course of the year. Ryan screamed and kicked until he saw Jaxon standing in front of him.

"Dad, get up!" Jaxon yelled.

Ryan couldn't move better yet face his own kids on how he treated their mother. Abbie ran into the room and at that moment Ryan knew he had to protect his kids and be the father they knew and loved. Ryan held both of the kids and promised them everything was going to be alright. They had so many questions that he couldn't answer.

"Dad, did you know mom was sick?" Abbie asked.

"I remember the last morning before school when she died she hugged us tight, kept telling us she loved us, and kissing us, I thought that was strange, but now I understand why," Jaxon said recalling Ava's last moment with them before school.

Ryan rubbed each of the kids' heads trying to understand.

"Mom didn't want us to know, she didn't want us to worry," Ryan said trying to reassure them. "Yes, Jaxon, now that I recall your mom's actions, she knew it was her time and wanted you both to know she will always be here and watching over you guys," pointing to their hearts.

Ryan sat there and held the kids until they fell asleep, he knew tomorrow would be tough for all of them. Ava's service was being held and her body would be cremated shortly after, just the way she wanted it. Ryan had no say what so ever in Ava's wishes or what she wanted because he was non-existent during that time of her life, which was something he would always regret. Ryan just hoped and prayed she was able to get and read his last text he sent to her "till death do us apart." Ava replied, but was it actually her if she was dying, he wondered.

Ryan looked at his phone and noticed all the missed calls and texts some were from family, friends, colleagues, and several from Sharon. Ryan wanted to text her back just to let her know he was okay, but figured he needed to keep the distance and focus on his kids. Ryan didn't need any distractions. Ryan turned his phone and television off then rested his head against the pillow hoping to get some shut eye.

---

Arriving at the church was one thing, seeing Ava one last time before the cremation was another. Ava requested that if the kids wanted to say goodbye they could see her before she was cremated per her cremation advisor. Ryan was able to go in with Jaxon and Abbie who took it well as he thought, but he thought the visit from Pastor Boeing helped them as well as the DVDs Ava prepared for all of them before she passed. Angela brought over the discs Ava prepared while she was sick.

The kids watched their disc yesterday, but Ryan decided to watch his later, after the service. Watching the disc with the kids and Ava explaining how sick she really was made him feel nothing, but guilt. All along the wigs Ava wore Ryan thought was her hair; the woman he married was gone, now Ryan has to raise Jaxon and Abbie as a single dad.

After viewing Ava's body earlier that morning, Ryan had to clear his head before going into the church. He sat in the car with the kids, massaging his temples. Sitting there he heard a tap on the window and saw it was Angela. Ryan and the kids finally got out of the car and they all walked in with Angela and Carl. Ryan greeted Pastor Boeing, who prayed with him and the kids before walking into this huge room where this big canvas of Ava stood. Ryan walked over and admired her beauty, smile, and, most of all, how happy she was. He touched the canvas as if she felt his hands. The kids leaned against Ryan as tears ran down his face. An usher brought over tissue as Ryan grabbed the kid's hands and took a seat while everyone watched on.

As people started entering there was also a projector showing of all of Ava's favorite memories. Ryan was even proud to see their wedding photos, the kids' birth, Ava's graduation, family, and just Ava being Ava with her girlfriends; boy, did she enjoy life.

Ryan noticed some familiar faces and some he didn't recognize. A news crew was outside as he whispered to Alisse to

*Love and War*

get rid of them. He was greeted by Brian, Dr. Patel, Ian and Sherry Baker, Brent, Andrew, Ricky, Ava's business associates, editor, agent, and a host of relatives he hasn't seen in years. One face he remembered was the white guy at Ava's party who gave the toast. He greeted Alisse, Angela, and the girls; then walked over to Ryan and the kids to give his condolences. Ryan was tempted to ask who he was to Ava and why he was there, but figured the timing was bad.

The service was starting as programs were being distributed. Abbie smiled when she opened the obituary and saw an old picture of her and Jaxon that read "My World" and a special message to them Ava wrote before passing. The way Ava sat everything up really made it easier on the kids, but harder for Ryan.

Pastor Boeing stood up he prayed, then read a scripture and touched a little on death and how to comfort those hurting. "Even though I walk through the valley of the shadow of death, I will fear no evil, for you are with me; your rod and your staff, they comfort me, Psalms 23:4 Ava who is comforted by The Lord our Savior is not suffering anymore nor does she have any more pain! Ava is safe in his arms, now and forever," Pastor Boeing spoke. "To Ava's grieving kids and husband, please don't be upset because you didn't know of her illness; be grateful for the reasons why she kept it from you. Ava had her way of doing things and keeping you all from worrying was her main priority....yes, Ava and I spoke on many occasions and she explained to me her reasoning I had to go along and respect her wishes, you see you don't have to worry about a funeral or any other expenses Ryan, Ava did this so you can focus on the kids and not worry, she'll always be with you and just know she was ready and she's safe. Church, let us pray," he said.

After moments of silence there were remarks by many of people who knew Ava, especially her agent, Elaine, and close friend. Angela, Karen, and Lisa read a touching poem, then the guy from the party stood and gave a brief remark on how Ava touched him; again Ryan was curious to know who that guy was. As he looked back, Ryan noticed Sharon sitting in the crowd and was furious at her for being there. He had to turn his head as she stared at him. Ryan hoped no one saw her in the crowd or they would have thrown her out!

Ryan's kids surprised him as they both stood up and shared special memories about Ava, which forced Ryan to stand and give his own remarks. Ryan stood up and was speechless at first, there was so much he wanted to say about the woman he wanted to spend his life with, but kept it brief. Ryan sat as he got really emotional; then found the kids comforting him.

Ryan looked back and noticed Sharon disappeared and was relieved. The closing of the memorial ended with the cremation advisor presenting Ryan and the kids with Ava's urns as she

## Love and War

requested to have her ashes spread over Lake Vale and a singing of Ava's favorite gospel song, *Way Down in the Valley*.

Ryan saw the kids finally smiling for the first time in days as people greeted them and talked about what a good person Ava was. Ryan saw the white guy who gave the remarks walking out the door and he quickly followed him.

"Hey!" Ryan called out as the gentleman turned around. Ryan didn't know what to say. "I noticed you at the party and now here, just curious to know…how did you know my wife?" Ryan asked.

"Hi, I'm Malcolm," he said as he extended his hand out to Ryan who then shook his hand. "I met Ava almost a year ago and we became really close friends. She was a really good woman, Ryan."

"I never told you my name?" Ryan said.

"No, but you're Ava's husband and she talked about you as well as everyone in that room, just know Ava died in peace…she had a friend to talk to as far as the divorce and her battle with cancer, I was there when you weren't," Malcolm said in a cocky way.

"Were you having sex with my wife?"

"Shouldn't you be in there comforting Abbie and Jaxon? But to answer your question Ryan, no. Ava was way too classy. Everything isn't about sex, but you on the other hand just lost way more," Malcolm shot back at Ryan as he began walking off.

249

Ryan walked behind him trying to figure out where he came from.

"So my wife confided in you?"

Malcolm kept walking to what looked like a Benz, he put his shades on, and turned to Ryan before opening his door.

"Yes, she did, she needed someone to talk to. Ava was a rare woman, but you couldn't see that Ryan. I cared for Ava dearly and yes, I will always love her. I'm glad she found peace Ryan," he said as he got in his ride and sped off.

Ryan walked back in the church to find everyone watching as they witnessed a scene. Ryan wasn't furious with Ava; he wanted to know was there something more to what Malcolm was saying. Honestly he couldn't be angry with anyone but himself; if anything occurred, he pushed her away and would regret that as long as he lived.

"What was that all about?" Alisse asked.

"Nothing, I know you've already met Ava's friend, Malcolm, I just wanted to know who he was!" Ryan said.

"Yes, Ryan, he was a very good friend to Ava," Alisse said not blinking her eyes once.

Ryan didn't say anything more; Elaine was also taking it all in. Ryan engaged with the others and greeted those who came. Abbie took Ava's canvas, while Jaxon stood with the pictures that all went with Alisse. Ryan was really ashamed he had no input on

*Love and War*

what was going on around him. Ryan heard a male voice and turned around.

"Sorry about Ava, man, I had no idea she was sick," Ricky said.

"Me either," Ryan said without realizing what he just said and why he was talking to Ricky.

"You didn't know she was sick?" Ricky asked.

"Excuse me," Ryan said walking off as he looked on.

Ryan wanted to get the kids and head home; this was really overwhelming to him.

Elaine walked towards him, "Ryan, tomorrow we all have to meet with the attorneys to go over Ava's will, 10:00 a.m." she said.

"We," he said.

"Yes, we," Elaine said and walked off.

Ryan knew something was off. Why was Elaine involved in Ava's will? *We? I was Ava's husband*, he thought. Ava still loved him and she knew he loved her, with all that was going on Ryan wasn't sure if he was interested in the reading of the will at that moment!

*Bianca Harrison*

## *Pushing Forward*

*I*t was very hard for Alisse to accept that Ava succumbed to cancer. Although she was in a better place, Alisse really wished she was still there. Ava was her sister, her best friend, and now she had no one she could talk to, she talked to Ava every day and her absence weighed on Alisse heavily. During Ava's sickness, Alisse promised her she would be a spokesperson for women and ovarian cancer.

Elaine and Alisse both went to see their gynecologist to perform several exams and tests for ovarian cancer and were both negative. Alisse learned that it was very hard to detect that type of cancer, but getting her regular annuals was a must. Alisse felt the need to stay on top of Abbie to make sure her chances were zero in getting ovarian cancer as well.

It had only been a couple of days since they'd said their goodbyes to Ava and a lot had transpired. Ryan was not happy

*Love and War*

with the outcome of Ava's will and he was trying to get it thrown out.

Ryan was divorcing Ava and had Ava taken off his insurance and cancelled her on their life insurance policy. Ava signed the documents Ryan asked her to sign, and they were turned in by Ryan. Ava didn't leave Ryan a dime and he thought he was entitled to it all; everything was to be divided between Abbie and Jaxon and would be disbursed when they each turned 21. Alisse had full control of the kid's accounts, Ava's books, and her movie royalties. Ryan was furious! Just the thought of him cashing in on the life insurance policy himself was sickening while all along Ava was sick.

Ava's last book, which was her memoir, was to be released next week and people were already raving about the book, which dished about everything leading up to her death and Alisse had an advance copy. Ryan would not be happy when he read it; after all he treated Ava like crap until those last couple of days when he had a change of heart regarding their divorce; by then it was already too late.

The kids were doing fairly well, but still trying to adjust without Ava who was their world. Abbie has become distant so Alisse encouraged her to go to counseling.

Alisse also thought it would be a great idea to promote Ava's book and movie herself. She would also bring Abbie, who could answer questions and sign the books on behalf of her mother.

Alisse liked the idea thanks to Ava's agent and publishing company.

Ava planned everything as she wanted it and so far so good. Alisse gave each of the girls their letters that Ava wrote for them; they all beamed at the thought of Ava writing them a letter before she died. Malcolm was given his letter prior as he called Alisse and cried. It was touching, he stated he never met anyone like Ava; he wished they had more time together.

*That's just like Ava, putting everyone else first!* Alisse thought, she was one amazing woman.

Malcolm also stopped by and stayed a while wanting to check in on how Ava's kids were coping and to talk about Ava's spirit. Meeting someone like her forever changed his life and Alisse could see why Ava cared about Malcolm – he was charming, a gentleman, and handsome.

Just as Malcolm was leaving, Ryan was pulling up with the kids just as Alisse was hugging Malcolm goodbye. Malcolm waved as Ryan ignored him, but the kids waved back.

"I see he's become a regular, Alisse, part of the family I would say," Ryan said trying to see what was really going on.

Feeding into his smart remark Alisse said, "Yes, he is a regular, more like family. Mom and I love him!" she replied cracking up.

Ryan didn't like that comment too well, "I don't want to see him near my kids, Alisse, I mean it!" He said acting as if

*Love and War*

Malcolm was a threat, but what Ryan was really mad about was Ava's will.

"Ryan, don't worry, he won't!" Alisse said ending that conversation.

Alisse could tell Ryan was agitated, hurt, feeling the pain he brought upon himself and the thought of him thinking he was going to live off of Ava's money. *You have to always treat people how you want to be treated*, she thought.

"Look, Alisse, I'm sorry, I'm just dealing with a lot. I put your sister through hell and realized when it was too late I made a mistake. I admit it…I made a mistake!" Ryan hollered.

Alisse told the kids to give them a minute. When they exited the room, Alisse gave Ryan the benefit of the doubt; she can forgive, but she can't forget how he treated her sister.

"I need you to help me with the kids; I'm sorry if you and Elaine hate me, how I treated Ava and flaunted my relationship with Sharon in her face wasn't me at all. Ava didn't deserve that! I really do miss her, Alisse, I do," Ryan said then broke down in front of Alisse.

Alisse noticed Jaxon standing at the door listening.

"Dad is okay, Jaxon, go check on your sister," Alisse told him watching Jaxon walk off.

"Ryan I forgive you, Ava forgives you….Ava realized you loved her and knew it when she passed," she said.

"But I wasn't there for her, Alisse, I wasn't!"

"Is it over with Sharon?" Alisse asked wanting to know.

"Yes....I broke it off that day," Ryan stopped then put his head down.

Alisse already heard from a friend that Ryan was over to Sharon's that Sunday, but Alisse wanted to hear what he had to say. Really Alisse wanted to comfort him, and then she thought about how he treated Ava. Did Ryan deserve her forgiveness? How can she push forward knowing her sister didn't deserve that type of treatment, Ava would have given anything to please Ryan, yet he cheated on her, then he asked her for a divorce and on top of that wanted half of her hard earned money to go along with it! God doesn't make any mistakes in life; therefore, Ryan will suffer the most. People often reap what they sow.

Alisse reached over, put her hand on Ryan's shoulder only to let him know she was there for him if he needed her.

Alisse just knew this was only the beginning for Ryan. He was going to endure more pain from his peers, family, and most of all, the media, when Ava's memoir hit the bookshelf....soon!

*Love and War*

# **Love and War**

**W**eeks had passed since Ava's passing and life hadn't been the same for Ryan. A huge slap in the face came after Ryan learned he wasn't entitled to any of Ava's earnings. Ryan never saw that coming unless they were already divorced.

He couldn't blame Ava for protecting her investments and all other assets, but truth be told, Ryan didn't know she had it in her; after all he was divorcing her. It wasn't about the money, Ryan just felt foolish because he looked stupid during the reading of the will when everyone else present was entitled to something.

Ryan was assured that his kids would be well off in their future – Ava did make sure of that – and Alisse was their trustee. Ryan, on the other hand, was left with nothing, but could he blame Ava? No!

Ryan watched the news for a bit, turned to CNN, and learned that Ava's debut movie would be released in a couple of weeks and that her memoir would be released this week. Ryan had no clue that Ava had written another book. He was so far up Sharon's ass, he had forgotten about his wife who needed him, therefore she returned the favor and forgot him in her will. Ryan had no clue about a memoir; he just thought it was another book until the CNN correspondent mentioned, *"Life is not a Fairytale (Secrets, Deception, and Ava's Marriage)*...an Ava tell all book!"

The correspondent had a preview copy and Ryan was stunned at the conversation and backlash. He heard Abbie call out for him and was frozen.

"This is Ava Decree's last and final book, released just before her movie hits theaters.. She died so young and so full of life, this book shares the triumphs of her personal life. I couldn't believe the way her husband treated her.....Ava was dying for God's sake…"

*"Oh, my God!"* was all Ryan could say. Ryan was now puzzled in what Ava revealed in her last book. Abbie walked into the room and he quickly turned off the television. Ryan's kids could not hear or read about whatever's in that book. Ryan brought nothing but shame to his family and this would ruin them knowing Ava was sick.

"Yes, sweetheart," he said to Abbie.

"Dad, I miss mom, it's not fair....I don't know what to do," Abbie said crying on his shoulder.

*Love and War*

Ryan comforted his daughter the best he knew how; he missed Ava, too. At night Ryan found himself talking to her and praying that she was listening.

"Mom is not far away, Abbie; she wants you to be strong. Although your mother is not here physically, she is here spiritually," Ryan said to her. He rubbed Abbie's shoulder as she glanced at the photos of Ava on the coffee table then laid her head back.

"Dad, why didn't mom tell us she as sick? I'm grateful she made us that video, but it's not the same," Abbie said

"I know, sweetheart, I know. I miss her, too, but I promise to do all the things your Mom did and to take care of you and your brother," he said letting Abbie know he would always be there for her and Jaxon.

Ryan took a leave of absence from work to get things back in order and to focus on the kids. He was giving the kids time to heal as well before sending them back to school.

Abbie got up from the couch and started to walk off. Ryan told her to check on her brother who was very quiet, which concerned him.

Ryan reminisced about Ava and how caring she was, when they first met, courted and the love they made....it was all gone. Ryan took Ava for granted something he never thought he would do. Ryan remembered the time when she first told him she was pregnant with Abbie, he was over joyed, he nearly scared Ava the death. *Just the little things*, he thought, *just the little things.*

Ryan poured himself a drink and went upstairs. Ryan closed the door behind him and put in the disc Ava made for him and sat there in tears when he saw her face on the monitor. Ryan tried to touch the television screen and caress Ava's face, but nothing. Ryan sat back in the recliner and listened to Ava talk about how sick she was and was shocked to learn the surgery Ava had prior was not a hysterectomy, "How did she keep that from me? Why wasn't I more attentive?" he asked himself.

Ava took her wig off revealing her head; she lost all her hair fighting for her life. Ryan could barely recognize his wife. Ava was frail, very thin, and pale. Although he saw Ava's appearance from watching Abbie and Jaxon's disc, this time around it seemed fresh because she was talking to him. Ava thought that Ryan had abandoned her; she lashed out at him for not fighting for their marriage *"You see, Ryan, I've been through hell...from losing my hair, chemo, radiation, and weight loss while you abandoned me for that whore!"* Ava hollered through the recording. Ryan paused the recording just to get himself together. If he could apologize a million times to Ava he would.

"I didn't mean to break up our home," Ryan yelled wishing she could hear him...."*to death do us part!*" Ava said and it was always something they said to each other.

*Love and War*

Ava yelled, screamed, and cried through all the pain telling Ryan he wasn't getting a dime of her money since he took her off the insurance policy, but through it all she still loved him. He felt so ashamed knowing all Ava asked for was for him to take care of their kids and their approval of whomever he married. Ava held up pictures Ryan hadn't seen in years, their wedding album, and reminded him of the life they had together before Sharon entered the picture. *"How could you, Ryan? You cheated on me and publicized your relationship in my face with her, something I tried to hide from our kids, but it was eating me up inside as well as this cancer. I'm fighting a battle between my love for you and a war with ovarian cancer, I can't win for losing,"* Ava said during her recording.

Ryan wanted to turn off the disc, but needed to understand what Ava was going through. Ryan didn't blame her, he understood what he put her through, but it was good to know that Ava did forgive him in the end. She blew Ryan a kiss through her tears, smiled and said, *"I love you, Ryan,"* and that was it.

Ryan broke down at that moment, beating himself up for what he had done, and during the process Ava was taken away from him. Ryan played the recorder over and over again just to hear Ava say, *"I love you, Ryan,"* he looked up only to find Abbie and Jaxon standing in the door way.

"Dad, you cheated on mommy?" Abbie asked.

At that moment Ryan had a blank stare from Abbie's question.

"Dad, did you hear Abbie? We heard what mom said. How could you?" Jaxon yelled and then walked off with Abbie right behind him.

"Kids, come here!" Ryan yelled trying to get up. "Jaxon, Abbie" he called out. Then the doorbell rang, but he wasn't in the mood for visitors.

Ryan ran downstairs and opened the door to Alisse.

"We need to talk," Alisse said holding up Ava's book the one he saw on CNN. "Wait, what's going on? You look a mess, eyes bloodshot red, and you smell like alcohol. Where are the kids?" Alisse asked in a hostile tone.

"Alisse now is not the time! What do you want?" Ryan yelled wanting her to leave.

"This, Ryan," Alisse said pointing to Ava's book. "Shit just got real, you got bigger problems…now I got to steer my niece and nephew away from the mess you made," she said, throwing the book at him.

*Love and War*

## ***Pain and Joy***

*T*he last couple of weeks had been hell. Angela picked up the phone a couple of times and dialed Ava to vent, and then realized she's no longer here. Angela wanted to go to her grave just to talk, and then realized Ava was cremated.

Angela tried to help Alisse put out fires and steer Abbie and Jaxon away from the media since Ryan was catching hell himself due to Ava's memoir. Angela read Ava's book from beginning to end like she always did and to tell you this was her best work simply because it was her own story. Things Angela didn't know she found out and truly understood why Ava dealt with Ryan and his infidelities.

Ava kept a journal throughout her life, which Angela never knew about that detailed her childhood, her father, marriage, author status, and her battle with cancer. She also inserted pictures that made it so much real.

Ava's father, whom she never talked about and who Angela assumed was dead, tried to molest her when her mom was sleep only to find Elaine behind him with a bat as he lay on top of Ava. Angela spoke with Alisse about the issue that led the girls to pretend their father was dead; they packed up moved and never looked back, something Ava pushed out of her mind. Although Alisse did mention their dad showed up to one of Ava's book signing, other than that, they have no clue where he is.

Angela sat at the table looking through the book while searching the net reading the comments from Ava's book when Carl walked in.

"Hey, beautiful," Carl said pecking Angela on the cheek. "What's going on or shall I ask how was your day?"

"Nothing, just reading the comments and reviews from Ava's book, other than that my day has been okay," she said.

"Speaking of that, everyone is talking about the book; I've read a couple of chapters and was baffled. Then the pictures of Ryan and Sharon got everyone at the office talking, we haven't seen Sharon since Ava's passing, I wonder how she feels about the situation," Carl said popping open a soda.

"That poor Sharon doesn't have any feelings because if she did she would not have slept with Ava's husband," Angela said just thinking about the time she last saw her at the restaurant. "Right now Ryan really does need some support…this is just

## Love and War

karma in how he treated Ava, she made sure he would get his while she's gone," Angela added.

Angela read online that Sharon contacted an attorney to get her pictures removed from Ava's memoir, but the only thing that could be done would be to blur out the faces going forward when they print books to send out since many have already been distributed. Angela didn't know why she did that, she was so proud to have Ryan on her arm in public while he was still married and opened her legs to him, so now she's embarrassed. *Just like a trifling female*, Angela thought.

"I think when and if Ryan decides to come back to work he will lose the contract he has with Sharon due to their involvement. I tried to tell him, but he was in way over his head," Carl said.

"The kids are coming over this weekend, if you don't mind," Angela said.

"Not a problem. I can imagine Ryan needs a break with all he's got going on. I called him, but he hasn't returned my call."

Angela heard Chrissy running down the steps yelling, scaring the shit out of Angela and Carl. "Mom, Auntie Lisa said answer your dang phone, Auntie Karen's on the way to the hospital to have the baby," Chrissy said catching her breath.

Angela jumped out the chair, searched for her phone, and realized it was in her purse on silent. "Shoot!" she said trying to retrieve it. Angela saw the missed calls and texts from both Karen and Lisa.

Carl was standing in the way; Angela pushed past him to find her shoes.

"Mom, can I go with you and see the baby?" Chrissy asked.

"Sure, baby, you better hurry."

"Babe, Chrissy don't need to see all of that stuff," Carl said seriously.

"Good Lawd, she's not going in the delivery room, Carl!" Angela said locating her shoes, keys, and purse as Chrissy was right behind her as they both headed for the door right towards the car.

---

*F*inally at the hospital Angela had time to call Alisse and tell her about Karen, who was in the delivery room having contractions and waiting for an epidural. Karen had dilated 5 centimeters so far and she was in so much pain.

Lisa walked over and asked Chrissy what she was doing there.

"I want to see my new relative," Chrissy joked.

Lisa then came over and sat beside Angela, "You know, I wish Ava could be here," Lisa said.

"Me, too, I think about her everyday Lisa...it's still so unreal," she said.

*Love and War*

They both got up and looked through the door at Karen who looked as though she was in major pain. Karen noticed them at the door and yelled, "I can't do this shit anymore!"

"Relax, Karen, and breathe," Angela said.

"Breathe my ass!" Karen shot back.

As they stood there, Angela noticed Abbie and Alisse walking towards her.

"Auntie Angela," Abbie said running into her arms.

"Hi, sweetheart, it's good to see you!" Angela said embracing her then Abbie embraced Lisa.

"Thank you for bringing her," Angela said to Alisse.

"We're taking Ava's place," Alisse said while smiling. Angela held her hand and smiled back just knowing Ava was already there.

Abbie spotted Chrissy and jetted. They all stood there and watched Chris hold Karen's hand; they all felt Ava's presence at that moment.

They sat briefly listening to Chrissy and Abbie talk nonstop while playing with their iPods. It was good to see Abbie smile. Moments later Chris called for the girls to come in the delivery room. Alisse stayed back with Chrissy and Abbie.

Angela and Lisa both entered the room; Angela held one hand, while Chris held the other. Lisa tried to relax Karen as she pushed. After a 20-minute battle of huffing and puffing, the baby finally popped out and what came after was a hot mess!

"It's a girl!" the nurse said.

Everyone was overjoyed as Lisa almost passed out and Karen lay back trying to catch her breath due to all that pushing. Chris cut the cord as Angela watched Karen wipe tears of joy from her face. The baby hollered as the nurse got her prepared and weighed her.

"She's healthy at 8 pounds and 5 ounces, she's a big girl," the nurse stated.

Chris took the baby from the nurse and kissed her. Not sure where Karen found Chris, but he was defiantly a keeper. Angela went to the door and motioned for Alisse and the girls to come in.

They all stood around watching Karen with her newborn and she was so happy. This was the same woman who didn't want kids, now she was happier than anyone had ever seen her. Angela heard Chris on the phone calling their parents to tell them the news and to bring his daughter by to meet her new sister.

Karen motioned for them all to come closer. "These are your aunties and cousins," Karen said to the baby. Chrissy and Abbie were excited.

"She's so pretty!" Chrissy said.

"What's her name?" Abbie asked.

"Ava... after your mom," Karen said.

Abbie put her hand over her mouth, and then turned to look at Alisse who held her.

*Love and War*

"Thank you, Auntie Karen. Mom would like that," Abbie said.

They all were emotional at that moment. "Ava is here with us I felt her and y'all know she would say....Karen push harder, dammit!" Karen said laughing.

They all laughed knowing she would say that, but at the same time be very proud.

"Another Ava, huh? I wonder if she's going to act anything like her," Alisse said.

"I hope not; we already got an Abbie who is the spitting image of Ava," Lisa said laughing.

They all stayed awhile, then gave Karen and Chris some space as other members of their family started to arrive. Angela was so glad all her girls found nice guys and were in a place in their lives where everything matters. Ava put them all together and for that Angela was grateful, she knew what true friendship was all about. The bond they all had and shared would remain as they stuck together, through the pain there is also joy.

*Bianca Harrison*

## *This Too Shall Pass*

*A*fter weeks of putting the finishing touches to Ava's last project, the moment was finally here. The premier and screening of Ava's debut movie, "This Too Shall Pass" was a reality.

Alisse had been working day and night to make sure her sister's legacy lived on through her books, her movie, her kids, and getting signed on to be a spokes person for Susan Wright, an ovarian cancer fighter who won her battle to ovarian cancer, launching the fight against ovarian cancer and making it a movement.

Alisse was so excited about being a spokesperson and also getting Abbie involved. Alisse promised Ava she would do everything in her power to end ovarian cancer, learning, understanding, and talking about the disease to help others become survivors since this disease is considered a silent killer among women.

*Love and War*

As Alisse selected the dress she was going to wear to the premiere, she noticed a text from Abbie and Jaxon. Alisse smiled as they sent photos of their attire, and they were ready to go. Alisse had to hurry because the limo would be there shortly. Alisse showered, then slipped on the red one-shoulder strap gown she had chosen to wear because red was Ava's favorite color and her Givenchy signature sandals to match. She also hired Ava's makeup artist from her 40th birthday party to assist her and do her hair. Elaine was already downstairs dressed and waiting for Alisse.

An hour later Alisse looked like a million bucks. The limo arrived just in time and Elaine had dozed off waiting for Alisse.

"Dang, what took you so long, the movie is probably over," Elaine said.

"Perfection, Mom, perfection" Alisse said grabbing her clutch.

They were heading to the AMC Hollywood Cinema where several of Ava's friends she worked with got invites, other authors, and family members. Several celebrities would also be in attendance. Alisse was nervous and sweating at the same time and Elaine noticed as well.

"Girl, what's wrong with you? You're shaking and ruining your makeup," she said.

"I don't know; I just wish Ava was here. Mom, I really hope this event turns out alright, I just wanna make her proud."

"Alisse, sweetheart, you already have," Elaine leaned over and put her hand on Alisse's knee. "Baby girl, you did well, don't worry so much. Ava is looking down at you clapping. I wish she was here, too, so she could see all that she was aiming for and finally did it."

Alisse pulled out the picture she had stuffed in her clutch of Ava and smiled, "She will always be with me."

Arriving at the venue was like a dream come true; Alisse had never been to a premiere and didn't know what to expect. There was press everywhere outside of the red carpet that met them as they exited the limousine. Fans were there as well, watching as people arrived while yelling. *This was something else*! Alisse thought.

"This is overwhelming," Elaine said looking at the crowd.

They exited and walked the carpet as photographers took their picture as they entered.

"Ava, Ava!" Alisse heard fans yell.

Alisse looked back to see Abbie, Jaxon, and Ryan exit their limo. Jaxon wore a shirt designed with Ava's picture and the word "MOM," the crowd went wild.

"RIP Ava, we love you," a fan said.

Elaine and Alisse waited for them to enter, a journalist tried to ask Ryan questions and Alisse heard one say, "Ryan, why did you do it?"

*Love and War*

Ryan smiled and kept walking. They all greeted each other and walked around the rope as it led them to the area.

"Alisse," Elaine called out, Ava's agent. "Hi, kids, Mama Elaine, and Ryan," she added as Elaine hugged Abbie and Jaxon.

"Everything looks nice," Alisse said.

"Thank you, it's all for Ava...this is a big deal, the movie was given five stars from the Global Chain Theater Production and that's great! This is Ava's moment," Elaine said.

They all continued to walk, take pictures, meet and greet, answer questions, then finally go into the venue to take their seats. The crowd clapped as they all entered; there was an announcer at the top. The theater was already jam packed with people. Alisse saw the girls and waved at them as they sat on the opposite end. There was an introduction before the movie as the lights went out and the movie began.

After watching the full one hour and fifty-three minutes of *This Too Shall Pass*, Alisse had tears in her eyes. Elaine was already wiping her face, everyone smiled as the ending was a special dedication to Ava. Ryan hugged both of the kids as he, too, was wiping tears from his face. The lights came on and Elaine, Ava's agent stood up to speak.

After the viewing, Alisse had a chance to sit down with different networks in attendance to help promote the movie and talk about the disease that took her sister. Afterwards they all went into the ballroom for food and drinks as Alisse met up with the girls to ask what they thought about the movie.

"Ava was great at producing behind the scene, I mean the actors and concept were a dream come true," Lisa said.

"Just imagine if Ava was here, what she could have become. Now it's up to us to make sure her legacy lives on," Karen added.

Angela was silent; Alisse knows she's thinking about Ava, so Alisse didn't interrupt her thoughts. As they all gathered for a toast, Abbie and Chrissy walked over with their cups of grape juice, holding them up. The girls counted down. Ryan, Carl, and the other fellas stood and talked; moments later laughter turned into frowns as Lisa noticed Sharon pushing her way through the crowd and handed Ryan some papers. She looked pregnant.

All Alisse heard was, "Sharon you got some nerve, how did you get in here anyway?" Ryan said.

"Just know you've been served, I'm suing Ava's estate for posting those pictures of me in her book without authorization!" Sharon yelled in Ryan's face.

"You won't get a dime! You're just a money hungry thirsty bitch Sharon, get outta here!" Ryan said in a tone that shook everyone.

"Bitch, Ryan?" Sharon said in anger.

Alisse then signaled for security to come throw Sharon out.

*Love and War*

"This bitch is something else! Ava is no longer here and she's still popping up at every event. I'm about to whoop her ass myself," Angela said.

Elaine realized where the commotion was coming from and told Sharon to leave or she would throw her out herself.

"Ryan, you will never see your child," Sharon yelled.

"Is she pregnant with your child?" Elaine said to Ryan demanding an answer.

"Dad, what did she just say?" Abbie asked him, not realizing she was still there.

"That baby is not mine!" Ryan said snapping at everyone looking in his direction.

Alisse directed security in Sharon's direction as Angela and Lisa walked behind her, people were starting to look in their direction from the commotion and Alisse felt embarrassed. Elaine was very upset as well.

Alisse heard a loud scream as people started running to see what was going on. As Alisse approached the crowd, she saw Sharon on the floor holding her stomach in pain. Sharon didn't notice the steps as she stormed off in a rage. Alisse looked on and shook her head in disgust. Angela and Lisa smirked only to turn around as they started walking back to the party as Alisse did the same. They all didn't give a damn. Alisse heard Sharon scream, moan, then cry...none of that fazed her, "Sharon got what she deserved!" Alisse said.

*Bianca Harrison*

## *Trouble Don't Last Always*

Sitting outside the waiting room and learning that Sharon lost the baby at 15 weeks was difficult in a way. Ryan was relieved, but felt bad in a sense. Ryan peeped in the room where Sharon lay there, dazed, then walked back to the waiting area.

The doctor said the baby would not have made it anyway due to the detachment of the placenta and the fall made it worse. Sharon blamed herself for causing a scene and being angry.

Ryan would not have come to the hospital if it wasn't for Carl. The kids went home with Alisse after the incident and Abbie wasn't speaking to him. Ryan needed to sit down and talk to the kids about this woman; too much had happened and the media put a spin on everything, making the situation worse than what it really was.

Ryan looked up and saw Sharon's mom walk by with Tiffany and one of her close friends. Ryan just really wanted to make sure everything was good so that he could leave. Carl texted

*Love and War*

Ryan and he texted back updating him on Sharon's status. Ryan then called Alisse to make sure the kids were okay; she kept the conversation short and sweet.

"Hi, Mr. Decree....Sharon would like to see you now," the doctor stated.

Ryan got up tempting to just leave. "Doctor, is she going to be okay?" he asked.

"Yes sir, she's just traumatized after losing the baby, give her some time...but she really needs your support right now," the doctor said and walked off.

Ryan headed down the hall, opened the door to Sharon's room, where all eyes were on him.

"The man of the hour," Sharon's mom said rolling her eyes.

"Hi to you as well," Ryan spoke.

Ryan looked at Sharon, then spoke with and hugged Tiffany. Sharon's mom had her friend take Tiffany out the room.

"Sharon, how are you?" he asked.

"Ryan, I lost our baby! So you can say I'm a mess right now," Sharon said.

"I'm sorry to hear that."

"Yeah, right, you're sorry for sure, but happy on the inside. You didn't want Sharon to have this baby, you're married for God sake!" Sharon's mom interrupted.

"Mom, please," Sharon said.

"Sharon, it's okay, I'm going to leave and I will talk to you soon," Ryan said trying to keep his mouth close from cursing her mom out. Ryan wasn't going to tolerate her bullshit and backlash any longer.

Sharon pleaded for him to stay as he walked towards the door, leaving her and her mom going at it.

Leaving the hospital was where Ryan planned to leave everything. He didn't plan on talking to Sharon soon; she had cost him enough. It was getting late and Ryan was exhausted.

Ryan drove home, thought about picking the kids up, but decided he'll deal with them tomorrow. He turned on the radio only to hear a radio personality who was at the event talk about the viewing party, Ava's debut movie, and to keep her family in their prayers. Ryan didn't hear any negativity for once, but how good of a mentor Ava was.

Ryan listened to the quiet storm on the radio when he heard Whitney Houston's song, *Why Does It Hurt So Bad*, he immediately broke down in tears and had to pull over. Ryan buried his face in the steering wheel as he sobbed. *If I could get one more chance with Ava, I would do things differently*, he thought. Ryan didn't even notice Ava or how sick she had become, and she was a woman that stayed in the same house as he did.

Ryan picked up the phone and dialed Carl a couple times then hung up, he called back, but he didn't answer. Ryan got himself together to continue driving. He weaved a few times as

*Love and War*

thoughts flashed back to Ava, if things were good between them he could have helped her beat that cancer, the thought of her going through that alone was beating him up inside.

Ryan drove until he reached the subdivision and pulled up in the driveway. He didn't bother pulling up to the garage, instead he got out and looked at the manicured yard, the flowers that were neatly placed, walked over and started pulling every single flower out the yard.

"Why? Why, God? Why did you take her from me, are you punishing me?" Ryan yelled kneeling down then started sobbing in the flower bed.

Ryan couldn't help how he was feeling and couldn't take it anymore. Ryan felt a hand on his shoulder as he jumped and turned around to Angela and Carl. Ryan then grabbed Angela's legs and started sobbing again.

"Ryan, please stop! You're going to wake the neighbors...I know you're hurting, but Ava wouldn't want you to feel sad, she loved you," Angela said.

Carl pulled Ryan up and hugged him.

"Man, Angela is right. Ava only wants you to be happy, she made that clear," Carl said.

Ryan stood there with tears, snot running everywhere and dirty.

"How could Ava want me happy when I cheated on her, Carl? I hurt her so bad and look what it has done to Ava, my family, and you think she wants me to be happy?"

"Yes, she does Ryan. You have no idea how much that woman loved you; at times it made me mad, but Ava's love was unconditional," Angela yelled at Ryan to pull himself together.

"Ryan, where are your keys? Let's get you in the house," Carl insisted.

Ryan gave Carl his keys and followed. Ryan was a mess. Life changes and the one person he could count on was no longer there.

Angela fixed Ryan a drink while he cleaned himself up then came back downstairs moments later.

"Guys, I'm sorry. I didn't mean to breakdown like that or you running to my aid. I had a moment and miss the hell out of my wife," he said to Angela and Carl.

"What are friends for? I knew something was wrong when you kept calling and hanging up, we all miss Ava, too," Carl said.

Ryan sat down as Angela handed him a drink. They all talked for awhile and recapped over the incident that took place at the viewing party. Ryan eventually would have to talk about Sharon's appearance sooner or later, so what better time than now.

Ryan looked around the room and everything was Ava, Ava, Ava; the room seemed to be spinning. He quenched his eyes

*Love and War*

and knew he felt her presence, so Ryan stood up and reached his hands out to her.

"Ryan, what's wrong man?" Carl asked.

"Ryan, what are you reaching for and what do you see?" Angela asked.

Ryan ignored Carl and Angela as he continued to look over in one direction and saw Ava's face from the picture on the wall and it was exactly Ava in the flesh walking towards him. Ryan started sweating as she got closer and didn't know what to say, he held his arms out for her, he smiled, called her name then walked over to meet her, then all of a sudden Ryan stumble's as he tripped and fell over on the couch.

## Catfight

Days passed since Ryan's melt down. Carl and Angela left him on the couch as Angela slipped a small dose of Benadryl in his drink. Ryan was going through the motions of guilt brought on by Ava's death.

Alisse stopped by Angela's as they talked about how well Ava's projects were doing since her death and Alisse being the spokesperson for the Susan Wright campaign against ovarian cancer. They also discussed the kids and how Ryan got them all in counseling, which Angela thought was great in dealing with all the issues that had surfaced.

"You know, Angela, I said it best: "what goes around comes around," Alisse said as she sat on the bar stool.

"You're right! I really feel sorry for Ryan, but I also felt my best friend's pain. You have to always treat people like you want to be treated," Angela said.

*Love and War*

"I do know and feel that Ryan is really sorry and that if he would have known about Ava's illness, he would have made some changes; but would she have to have been sick for him to change, I wonder," Alisse said as she thought about the situation.

"That is something we will never know, but I do know Sharon thought she would end up with Ryan and what all Ava had, you see how quickly the tables turned on that home wrecker. God don't play! There is never a happy ending for women who open their legs to married men, you feel me?" Angela said to Alisse who gave a high five.

Angela cleaned the kitchen and grabbed her purse so they could both head over to the spa and meet the other ladies. Angela was overdue for a back massage.

Alisse talked nonstop on the drive to the spa and Angela wanted to tell her so badly to hush just for a moment so she could listen to the radio, but decided to let her babble. For once, Angela could not wait to get to the spa. She then noticed Karen and Lisa as they approach them. Lisa checked them all in as they waited for a moment, then followed the Chinese lady into a room of luxury and changed into their attire that was laid out for them to put on. There was a room full of chocolate, appetizers, fruits, water bottles and a bottle of wine.

When Angela went out into the hall on the other side, there was a fish aquarium, they all headed to the rooftop that over looked the shores of Lake Tahoe, it was nice. This was Angela's first time at this spot and she could see why it cost so much as everything was gorgeous.

There was a section just for them with massage tables, chairs, masseuses, a facial area, foot scrub, and a nail technician on deck, plus a table full of appetizers, desserts, and drinks.

"I could get use to this," Karen shouted running a strawberry through the chocolate fountain.

"Yeah, this is where all my money went, but I won't complain," Angela said.

They all headed to the massage table as the masseuses were ready for them. As the masseuse dug deep into Angela's back, she started drifting off until Alisse started babbling again, then the conversation changed as Lisa started talking about crazy shit that had them all laughing out loud.

The spa outing was just what they all needed. They all agreed to do it more often, since Ava's death they all couldn't get it together, but knew they had to continue living and keep her memory alive.

"So, how is baby Ava, Karen?" Angela asked.

"She's good, growing so fast. I wish I could pause time. My baby girl is not a baby anymore," Karen said.

"Naw, Karen, let her grow up; you already talking about you don't get no sleep!" Lisa said while laughing and throwing a grape at Karen.

*Love and War*

Shortly after the massage Angela headed over to get a facial and a manicure. She thought it felt so good to relax for a moment until Angela heard Alisse talking Lisa's head off as they both were getting a foot scrub, while Karen was laid out in the tanning bed.

Angela glanced up and noticed how Lisa was taking in one wine glass after another while she tried to tune Alisse out. Angela laughed and placed the cucumbers back on her eyes shaking her head.

Hours later they all felt rejuvenated and decided to have dinner on the mountain top before heading back. They had to hurry and get dressed because there was another party waiting to use the room to change. Angela was dressed first and decided she would go check them out and wait in the lounging area.

Angela went to the front desk, picked up their care package that the staff gave to all parties after their visit and signed them all out. As Angela turned around she bumped into Sharon and some friends.

"Oh, sweetie, I'm sorry...oh, I remember you, Lisa, right?" Sharon said.

"No, it's Angela."

"That's right, how could I forget?" she said grinning like something was funny.

Angela smiled at her and thought some people you just have to play nice to, but this chick was different.

"How is Ryan? The baby? Oh, that's right, I remember, you didn't end up with either," Angela said bursting her bubble.

"Oh, that was cold!" one of Sharon's friends said.

"You are such a bitch!" Sharon said in anger. "How dare you bring up my baby? Ask Ryan about us," she mouthed off looking pathetic.

"Your ass just seems to pop up everywhere these days Sharon, kinda like a popcorn whore!" Angela said.

"Oh, I got your popcorn whore!"

At that time the rest of the girls approached the area.

"Is there a problem?" Lisa asked.

"No, just playing catch up with this home wrecker," Angela said.

"I'm not going to take anymore of your name calling and bullshit, Angela! You don't know me. I would hate to bust your ass in the mouth!" Sharon said as she started getting loud in the lobby showing out for her girls.

"Child, please. I know that you're a trifling bitch that will do anything to fuck another woman's man!"

Angela must have struck a nerve; Sharon slapped the shit out of her. Before Angela knew it, she kneed Sharon's ass in the gut. Management ran out just in time because it was going to be on between Sharon's crew and Angela's.

"I'll see you in the streets," Sharon yelled as they were whisked away to their room. At that moment they all exited the spa

*Love and War*

standing in the front entrance as Alisse said she forgot her makeup bag and went back in. Angela was so frustrated she wanted to go in and whip Sharon's ass for the sake of Ava. Lisa stays ready, and Karen just goes with the flow these days.

"Alisse's ass didn't forget her makeup bag, it's right here!" Lisa said pointing to it.

They all went back in because Angela had a feeling that with Alisse being Ava's sister she was going to make sure Sharon knew it. The front desk clerk called the management staff as they hurried to find Alisse.

Lisa opened the door to the changing room and as Angela thought: Alisse and Sharon were neck and neck.

Everyone stood by and listened, Angela watched Sharon's friends closely in case one of them wanted to jump bad.

"Too bad your sister isn't here to defend herself," Sharon said to Alisse wondering why she was in her face.

"It's too damn bad, but that's okay, Sharon. As I recall my sister was too white to be married to a black man. As I recall that ass of yours wasn't good enough to keep the same black man you've opened your legs to," Alisse said to Sharon with a smirk on her face.

"Damn, I know that stung!" Lisa hollered.

"Another thing, Sharon, what's your take on interracial relationships? Is it supposed to be black date only blacks and white date only whites? Huh?" Alisse asked boldly.

"Oh my," Angela heard someone say.

"Girl, I'm not going there with you, you don't know the story and you're clearly angry over something you know nothing about," Sharon said raising her voice.

Before Alisse could speak, a knock was at the door and the Chinese lady peeped in stating the masseuses were ready for Sharon's party.

Angela signaled for the girls, but Alisse wouldn't budge. Angela figured that woman was not worth their precious time. They've already spent enough energy on her as it is.

"That's what I thought!" Alisse said. "Ladies, don't let this chick fool ya, I know all too well," Alisse said to Sharon's friends and walked out, the girls all followed in a single file line like puppies.

"I hear them bitches in there talking," Lisa said.

"Let'em talk, hell," Angela said.

They all burst out in laughter at what just happened, wow what a day. Angela couldn't stand that damn girl, Sharon just did something to her. Angela cringed at females like her.

They jumped on the shuttle that transported them to the mountain top. The breeze felt good. Angela looked at Alisse and smiled.

"Did you want to whoop Sharon's ass?" Karen asked Alisse.

*Love and War*

"Oh hell yeah, just for my sister's sake. I was tired of her mouthing off like she was a victim. I couldn't sit back and not say anything, I wanted to hit her, but know I would have gone to jail since I went back in there like a fool," Alisse said.

"Hell, I wouldn't have cared; y'all asses would have bailed me out," Lisa said laughing. "I was waiting on something to pop off."

"Girl, I spent all my money at this luxury spa, ain't nobody got time to be getting you outta jail," Angela said.

"You just better be glad she slapped your ass first and it got stopped before you really went in on her ass or you would have needed me to come get you out of jail," Lisa said laughing.

"That's right," Karen said.

Angela shook her head. They made their way to the mountain top and the set up was nice. After that encounter with Sharon, Angela couldn't wait to sip something. They all made a toast to Sharon's dumb ass and was glad they didn't have to beat nobody down!

"To the whores all over the world, karma is a bitch!" Lisa yelled.

"Oh, hell naw," Angela said.

As they downed a bottle in a quick five minutes. Angela couldn't help but notice that this crew was alright with her. *My girls*, she thought, *my girls*.

*Bianca Harrison*

## *When Guilt Sets In*

After the girls all had dinner on the mountain top they ended up at Sax Contemporary Lounge to hear some live music where the Blueprint band was playing. Alisse thought it was a nice and relaxing evening with the girls after all the chaos that happened earlier.

Alisse looked around the room and saw how couples were reacting to one another as well as the singles that were out prowling. The band was playing while she sat and looked at the crowd not even noticing the guy standing in front of her asking for a dance.

The gentleman held out his hand as Alisse said, "No, thank you." He proceeded to ask the other girls then finally moved to the other table after no one budged.

Lisa got up went to the bar as Karen kept texting Chris and checking on baby Ava.

"What's wrong Alisse?" Angela asked.

*Love and War*

"Nothing, I'm just chilling," Alisse said as she continued looking around. Alisse felt like her life died when Ava died. Everything around Alisse reminded her so much of Ava. Alisse couldn't fill her shoes, but she was trying so hard even filling in her position with her girls.

Alisse looked at Karen and wondered what she thought of her, how she really viewed Ava. Then there was Angela who had it all together, how did she and Ava become best friends, what did they have in common and the same for Lisa, she was a free spirit just like Ava, but rough around the edges in ways.

Alisse started to get teary eyed and knew this was not the place or time. Ava has been gone for awhile now, but she seemed to always be with her wherever she went.

Angela slid over and pinched Alisse, "Shake it off, Ava is okay" she said.

Alisse looked at her and smiled, "How did you figure I'm thinking about Ava?"

"Girl, I know that look and besides your ass is about to cry!" She said laughing. "I find myself doing the same thing and I have to shake it, I miss my girl, but know she would want us to be happy."

One thing for sure, Angela was right. Alisse tried to enjoy the band and free her mind.

Alisse glanced at her phone for any messages and read the text from Justin on how much he missed her, and then the one from

291

Abbie begging Alisse to come get her, she refused to stay with her dad. There was one text after the other from Abbie. Alisse tried calling her, but got her voice mail instead. She tried Jaxon, he picked up but Alisse could barely hear him.

Alisse asked Angela could they leave since she rode with her, but Karen said she'll take Alisse because she had to leave and get to her baby. Alisse hugged Angela and Lisa and exited the Lounge with Karen.

Not sure what was going on, Alisse had to get the kids, she promised Ava she would look after them. Karen drove, they talked briefly, and the ride back seemed like it took forever. Alisse was finally picking her car up from Angela's heading over to Ryan's place.

Alisse called and notified Justin of her plans before heading home. She then called Ryan not knowing what to expect, but he didn't pick up. After driving for awhile she pulled into the driveway and ran to the door.

"Who is it?" Ryan asked.

"It's me, 'Lisse."

Ryan opened the door with a wife beater, sweats, and hair all over his face smelling like he'd been drinking.

"What are you doing here?" He asked.

"Abbie called me to come get her. I tried calling you. What's going on Ryan?"

*Love and War*

"You tell me, you run over here every time the kids call like you're their mom, Alisse!" he said being a smart ass.

"Yes, I do, Abbie and Jaxon are my sister's kids!"

Ryan got in Alisse's face, "They are my kids, Alisse; whatever I say goes! My wife birthed them, not you!" he hollered.

"You mean the dead wife you cheated on Ryan?" Alisse yelled back.

"Is that all you got, Alisse? Ryan cheat, cheat, cheat, cheat, cheat! Damn you!"

"Stop it you guys, stop it!" Abbie hollered as she entered the room hearing every word that was said.

"I'm sorry, baby girl, I'm sorry," Ryan said as he tried to hug Abbie. Abbie then pushed him away. Jaxon came down with an overnight bag and said he was going with Alisse.

Alisse asked the kids what was going on. Abbie stated their dad was drinking more and gets angry. Abbie also said she watched the tape Ava made for Ryan and what her Dad did to her Mom broke her heart.

"Abbie why did you watch that video? That was for your Dad," Alisse asked.

"Auntie, I already knew. I heard it when Dad played it for himself and the lady showed up at the movie premiere. I had to see Mom and hear it for myself coming from her," Abbie said crying.

Jaxon took the bags, didn't mutter a word, and headed for the car. Alisse could tell Ryan's affair and poor choices were affecting the kids. Alisse told Abbie to go to the car so she could talk to Ryan.

"Abbie, Jaxon, where the hell do y'all think you're going?" Ryan said. "I make the decisions around here!"

"Kids, keep walking," Alisse said.

Alisse closed the door and told Ryan to sit his ass down. He argued with her back and forth, until he gave in. Finally he sat down and listened to what she had to say.

"First of all, you are Jaxon and Abbie's father, but as Ava had it in her will, if you are unfit, or can't take care of them, I have the right to take them from you. Remember Ryan, the kids have the option to live with me if they want to," before she could continue Ryan cut her off.

"So you're doing me a favor, is that what you're saying?"

"As a matter of fact, I am. Look at you: you're drinking yourself to death. You don't know how to interact with those teenagers of yours. They are so torn about your affair, you don't even see it."

Ryan got up, wiped sweat off his face and headed towards Alisse. She stopped him dead in his tracks.

"You just have my kids back in this house by tomorrow afternoon, you hear!" Ryan yelled.

Alisse looked at him and turned and walked out the door. This was an issue all by itself.

*Love and War*

Alisse cooked the kids breakfast and promised to talk to them soon. Too much was going on with Ryan that he needed to take care of himself before he could take care of Abbie and Jaxon.

Alisse knew Abbie was only acting out as she knows how and Jaxon just held everything in until he exploded. Alisse wanted the kids to release whatever emotions they were holding on to, so that they could move forward.

Jaxon walked into the kitchen looking just like his mom and sat at the table.

"Good morning" he said.

"Morning sweetheart, how did you sleep?" Alisse asked.

"Good, but think I slept on the wrong side…my neck hurts."

Alisse fixed him a plate of his favorites, just then Abbie walks into the kitchen looking tired with her hair all over the place.

"Good morning, Auntie and Jaxon," she said.

"Good morning, how did you sleep and why didn't you tie your hair up?" Alisse asked.

"Good…at least Dad's not here to yell like he does all the time," she said.

Alisse fixed Abbie a plate, sat down with the kids and told them to start talking.

"Nothing is the same since Mom died," Jaxon said.

"Dad is angry all the time because Mom didn't tell him she was sick. I ask him about that lady, Sharon, and he just goes nuts," Abbie said. "I even heard him talking to himself about how she ruined our family and he can never get mom back because of her," Abbie added.

"Is that right?" Alisse said curious to how Ryan was really handling Ava's death.

"Dad is drinking more and more…he is not the same person. I can't stand to be around him. I want him to get help." Jaxon said.

"When I see that Sharon lady, I'm going to beat her ass, Auntie!" Abbie said.

"Abbie, watch your mouth!" Alisse snapped.

"Auntie, she is a whore that tried to tear our family apart. She slept with Dad while he was still married to Mom. So, yes I'm going to beat her ass!"

Alisse looked at Abbie and couldn't believe what she was hearing. What is the world coming to? Her mouth, her anger, and frustration were at another level. Cursing? Alisse was shocked.

"Abbie, watch your mouth! Your Dad's situation has nothing to do with you. Things happen, but you have to let adults handle their problems, not you," Alisse said snapping at her.

Alisse talked to the kids some more and knew she needed to talk to Ryan. She excused herself from the table and phoned him in the other room. Ryan sounded much better than he did last night.

*Love and War*

He agreed to come over so they could talk and hopefully get everyone back on track.

The kids cleared the table as Alisse told them to, and to get dressed. Their Dad was coming over. They weren't pleased, but Alisse really needed to help them through this transition.

As time went by, Alisse got dressed and phoned Angela, who left her a message earlier to see if everything was okay since she left the Lounge in a hurry. Alisse filled her in as she wanted to rush over, but she told her to stay put, that she'd let her know how everything goes after they sit with the kids. Moments later the door bell rang and it was Ryan. The kids didn't bother letting him in, so Alisse had to get the door.

Ryan greeted the kids and gave them both a hug before sitting. He looked sober and clean, which shocked the kids. Alisse motioned for Abbie and Jaxon to take a seat as she sat across from them. Alisse started the conversation. She had written down notes based on what she gathered from the kid's conversation with her and handed a copy to Ryan.

As Ryan looked over the sheet, his eyes started to tear up; he immediately broke down in front of them all and cried kneeling over in his own tears. Alisse didn't know what to do watch him or grab some tissue, but all she could see was the image of her sister crying to her about how Ryan was treating her. Ryan looked remorseful as he was crying to his kids. Maybe Alisse was still bitter on how he hurt Ava because she didn't go running to his aid.

Alisse sat there emotionless and watched in anger, but her God wouldn't let her stoop that low. She grabbed some tissue and went to Ryan's side, she tried to comfort him the best she knew how.

Ryan looked at the sheet again and apologized over and over to the kids as he promised to be a better dad and not to drink again.

"I'm just trying to deal with Ava's death the best I know how. I hurt your Mom badly and now I'm hurting you guys. I'm sorry, I'm so sorry!" he cried out.

Jaxon hesitated at first, then finally got up and hugged his dad. Alisse looked over at Abbie, who was also crying. She finally joined her brother and gave Ryan a hug.

"I know I haven't been the best father lately, and I'm sorry. Jaxon, I haven't been that man you look up to, and Abbie I haven't been the man you need in your life. I love you guys so much and we need each other to get through this, you hear?" Ryan said.

Alisse watched as the kids comforted Ryan, and then she exited the room to give them some space. She picked up Ava's picture off the console table and embraced it as if she was standing next to her.

"Sis, I sure do miss you," she mumbled, as Alisse heard Ryan tell Abbie she reminds him so much of Ava. *That she does*, Alisse thought.

*Love and War*

## **Moving On**

Sharon stopped by the house to tell Ryan she's been transferred from her job and to see how he was holding up. Although the kids were in school, Ryan tried to be cordial to her, but it was something about her being brave enough to stop by the place where Ava once lived. It was disrespectful to not only him, but to Ava as well, he thought.

    Therapy was really helping Ryan because he would have slammed the door in Sharon's face, but he had to remember that she was also a victim and didn't know how to let go of what they once had.

    Ryan stood in the door as Sharon talked, she told him that she dropped the lawsuit against Ava's estate, about the incident at the spa with the girls, and that she was truly sorry about Ava. She apologized for causing pain and only wanted peace, but couldn't understand how Ryan left her out in the cold after losing their baby and Ryan thought, *Here we go again.*

"Sharon, I'm truly sorry for my part in our affair, I did love you. Right now my life has totally changed, my kids are my first priority and not only have you been through hell, my name is still being dragged through the mud by the media. I really do apologize," Ryan said to her as nice as he could be.

Sharon stood there teary eyed. She wanted to say something, but stood quiet for a brief moment.

"Ryan, I loved you with all my heart and I still do. I had even started making wedding plans. I just couldn't understand how things went so right, but ended up to be so wrong. Tiffany started calling you Dad and that meant a lot to me, but yet you abandon us. I really don't know how to deal with this," Sharon said.

Ryan reached out and hugged Sharon because he really felt sorry for her, but at that moment he couldn't give Sharon what she wanted or deserved. Ryan was in a place to honor Ava and his kids, even if it meant being single for a very long time.

"God put us in positions sometime to make us realize things, even mistakes. Sharon you are the most loving and caring woman I know, but I'm not the man for you. In due time, you will forget all about me. Time, sweetheart, time," he said.

"That's easy for you to say. I guess Ricky was right about you after all," she said.

"I guess so, whatever that means. Look I have to get back in and start dinner, kiss Tiffany for me; and Sharon, I truly hope you find the happiness you deserve. I really do mean it, you're a

## Love and War

good woman," Ryan said as he kissed her on the cheek before turning around to walk back in the house.

"Thanks, too bad it isn't you Ryan, too bad," Sharon said as she headed towards her car.

Ryan looked out the window and noticed Sharon sitting in her car crying. He knew he hurt her just as much as he hurt Ava. He looked up at Ava's picture and thought there wasn't a woman in this world that could take her place. Had Ryan known Ava was sick; things would have been a lot different.

Sharon finally drove off. As she looked back, she caught Ryan looking out the window. He jumped back and took a call from Carl.

"Hey, man. How are you?" he asked.

"I'm good taking it one day at a time," Ryan said keeping it short.

"Good to hear, you up for dinner later?"

"Nah, I'll have to pass, I'm about to start dinner for the kids. How is work?" Ryan asked wondering.

"It's work, a lot of whispering about you know what, but nothing major. So when are you coming back?" Carl asked.

"I'm not sure man. They took the contract I had with Sharon and gave it to Ricky, after everything exploded in the headlines, so I'm not sure if I even want to come back to work. I really need to focus on the kids."

"What? Man, I had no idea! No wonder Ricky's walking around here like he is the man, damn!" Carl said.

Ryan listened to Carl a bit, then his mind started wondering, how would he make it staying at home? Ava didn't leave him a dime, but he also had a couple of options. Ryan just didn't want to go broke in the process.

"Look man, I have to go, I'll call you soon," Ryan said as he clicked the end button on his phone.

Ryan sat there contemplating his next move. Ryan thought about starting his own company, then the more and more he thought about it, he wanted to work with Alisse on Ava's projects and get more involved with cancer awareness. Ryan didn't know how Alisse would feel, since they hadn't seen eye to eye lately, but it was worth a try.

Ryan owes it to Ava to do right by her in death as he couldn't as her husband. The guilt was weighing heavily on him as the months went on.

Ryan still thinks about her pretty face. Ava always reminded Ryan of the actress Eva Mendes, with her almond complexion skin tone. Ryan told her that when he met her at the bank, she would be his wife and that she was.

Ryan got so caught up in his thoughts that he didn't hear his phone ring. It was Angela, who was just checking in. Ryan didn't answer because he didn't feel like talking to her, but he did phone Alisse.

*Love and War*

Alisse agreed to hear about Ryan's idea and what he wanted to do; and, of course, she thought it was about Ava's money, not her legacy. He pleaded his case to Alisse; she wasn't cutting Ryan any slack. Ryan wanted to strangle her ass through the phone, but he kept his cool since she was Ava's sole executor. Ryan felt like it wasn't a point in talking to Alisse; she was protecting Ava and didn't give a damn about his feelings.

Ryan hung up feeling like crap, "Asshole!" he mumbled.

How could Alisse not let him be involved in Ava's projects? Alisse was like a sister to Ryan once, just like Ava was once his wife, he just knew time played a part in everything, if only he could get that back…time…it was everything and more.

## *Epilogue*
### *One Year Later*

One year later after Ava's death, Ryan was finally at a place where he had found peace. His life had changed dramatically. As Ryan left the podium after giving a speech in front of hundreds of cancer survivors, he felt a lot has been accomplished.

Joining Alisse and being a spokesperson on Ava's behalf had also brought Ryan and the kids closer. Abbie was now 14 and Jaxon, 13, and they kept him busy nonstop. Ryan was more involved with Jaxon and his baseball as well as Abbie and her basketball.

Ryan had been celibate for over a year and it was hard, especially for a man. He hadn't run into Sharon nor had he heard from her. Ryan prayed that she found happiness wherever her heart opens. Ryan hurt her as well as everyone else and hoped she, too, found peace.

*Love and War*

On the other hand, Ryan was not looking for a mate. He'd gotten back into the church and talked with Pastor Boeing on a daily basis. Between projects and the kids he didn't have time to date. Ryan saw Ricky from time to time at church, but not often. Alisse and Elaine had forgiven him and they all agreed to move forward and bury the past.

Ryan visited Lake Vale and talked with Ava on a regular to clear his mind. The kids and Ryan still celebrate Ava's birthday, their anniversary, and Mother's Day, which would never change. One day Ryan would see her again and he promised not to let her slip away. Ryan learned that it was the small details of their lives that really mattered the most, especially in a relationship. When the time came and it felt right, maybe he'd find someone just like Ava, but in due time. Right now Ryan embraced life and all that it had to offer while he kept Ava's legacy alive.

## *Ovarian Cancer*

*Ovarian Cancer accounts for about 3% of cancers among women, but it cause more deaths than any other cancer of the female reproductive system. Please learn more about the causes of Ovarian Cancer and what you might be able to do to lower your risk.*

*#LetsFindaCure*
*#FightCancer*

## *Acknowledgments*

Thank you my Lord and Savior Jesus Christ for another book completed. All praises going up. This book was a breeze. No writers block or struggle with this one just putting it all into perspective.

To my family, spouse, and kids, thank you the long way. Love you all to pieces!

Also a big thank you to those that played a major part in getting this book to the forefront - Jennifer Swartz (editor) thank you once again for delivering.

Octavia Sims, Demetria Hayes, Keisha Thornton, Joshua Dickerson, Shirley Aldridge, Nicholas and Gisela Johnson, Edifyin Graphix, Createspace, distributors, bloggers, vender's, book clubs, and especially all readers: thanks for a great support system.

To other authors and friends that I've bonded with during my writing journey - thanks for being supportive and welcoming me with open arms to this industry.

Also a special thank you to all that has supported me from the beginning and continuing to support me as I keep pushing, I appreciate all the reviews, emails, and most of all the encouraging words.

Much love,

*Bianca*

Bianca is the author of *Someone to Call My Own*. Born and raised in South Georgia, she currently resides in North Georgia with her family. For more information visit her website at www.authorbiancaharrison.com or feel free to email the author at authorbiancaharrison@gmail.com.

Made in the USA
Charleston, SC
11 December 2014